TO HEAR THUNDER

By William Clark

Table of Contents

Chapter One

Kansas 1939

The sheriff's body had lain on its side, near the running board of his Model A without even a twitch for a solid hour now. Sheriff Dawes had used his own truck on Morton County business for months saying that folks felt less threatened in these hard times when he drove up unannounced in his truck as opposed to the county car. High above, a cloudless bright blue sky carried the sound of crows drifting in the hot breeze. Down below, half-hearted gusts stirred up small dust devils beside the body, *maybe a weak attempt on God's part to pick him up*, thought Penny wiping the last dirt track of tears away from his face. Another gust of hot wind blew across the porch carrying a thin grit of dirt, a dust that he could taste.

Over the last several months living with the dust had become familiar. There had been no way to avoid it. It came through the cracks in the walls and up through the floorboards of the house like a Biblical plague in Egypt, a story Penny's father liked to tell regularly. A scourge drifting in the constant wind, it coated everything with a fine talc. Food (what little there was), clothes, bedding, hair, everything was covered with it.

Penny looked over at the body of his father lying half in and half way out of the front door, thick dark blood oozing out from under him and dripping through the cracks in the porch. He had moaned once after the buckshot from the sheriff's shotgun had knocked him off his feet, spraying small bloody holes from his chin to his belly.

Penny had been sitting on the porch when Sheriff Dawes had driven up. He had watched him carry the papers in one hand and the shotgun in the other, a familiar movement seen a hundred times at a hundred other different farms. Transfixed by the deadly encounter, Penny watched as his father and Sheriff had begun shouting at each other the second Amon had pushed open the screen door with the barrel of his shotgun.

"You get off my land, Bob. I've been here my whole goddamned life," shouted Reynolds. Penny had never heard that odd high-pitched tone in his father's voice before. It had been more of a sobbing, desperate plea than a threat, a tone that immediately made Penny cry. It had been the sound of absolute brokenness. Penny hadn't been able to move, hadn't been able to speak knowing that something was ending here, something that could not be stopped. Terrified, he had watched the veins on his father's neck bulge in anger as he had continued to shout at the Sheriff who had begun backing up.

"Amon, you put that goddamned gun down. I'm the law here and I have a job to do."

"I won't say it again, Bob," Amon had screamed stepping forward. "Those papers mean nothing to me." Penny had never seen his father this way. It was as if all the pain, all the misery and loss of the last year had been coming out in his father's voice.

Amon Reynolds had been born in the house he was about to die in, a fourth generation dirt farmer who was known in the area for his honesty and kindness to those who had less, which nowadays was just about everybody they knew. The man who stood on his porch in overwhelming pain and desperation clutching a shotgun was someone Penny had never seen before. There had been a giddy terror in the hot air, a wild rage that neither man could stop. It swirled in the dusty air as Amon had raised his single barrel twelve gauge, the same shotgun he had shot a wild turkey with last November just down the road, the same shotgun that had stayed secured above the stove for years, an object of stability in a world that was anything but stable.

Theirs was the last farm on the two-mile stretch of road just outside of Elkhart, Kansas, that still had people living there. Their neighbor, old man Bartle, had hung himself in his barn six months earlier, unable to dig out of a black depression from losing all his stock and crops to the wind and dust. He had only seen one way out. In better days his wife had always offered fresh cornbread when Penny walked by on his way home from school. The whole place burned to the ground two weeks after they cut the old man out of the rafters. Some say it was Mrs. Bartle's last act of defiance to the bank just before she left with her relatives to places unknown.

Jessup Hargrove, who owned thirty wind-scarred acres on the other side of the road, just disappeared one night with his wife Dora and their two daughters Cora and May. May was Penny's age, and they had spent more than a few long days together hunting jack rabbits, sage hens, or just about anything else that would go into the pot. At fifteen, May looked like her mother, tall for her age, rail thin, with dark eyes, eyes that carried a twinge of sadness and want even when she smiled or laughed. To yearn for something you will never have marks a person early and deep, even a child.

was full of coins and folded money. They had given what they could, the community's way of saying good-bye.

On the ride back to town, Penny kept a stony silence, the air heavy with the things neither wanted to talk about. The pastor had told the county authorities that the boy would be staying with him and his family until the case was cleared. At first, Steven Harper, the County Commissioner, had objected, but after several visits from angry residents of the community, he decided that antagonizing an already angry and openly hostile bunch of dirt farmers in these rough days would not be a good idea. There had been enough bloodshed.

"Penny, I know leaving here is a hard thing, but I'm sure your aunt in Des Moines is going to be real glad to see you," announced the Pastor, trying to lighten the mood.

Penny thought for a moment. "Don't know her. Never met her."

"Well, she sounds like a very good woman in her telegram. They have a nice home in the city with indoor plumbing and electricity. Sounds real nice. I think they even have a telephone."

Penny spat brown phlegm from the dusty ride out the window. "I ain't going. Don't know those people," he replied looking at the pastor. "I'm sixteen today. I'll go my own way."

The pastor nodded. "Well, Penny, I know you're sixteen but in the State of Kansas you're considered a minor, which means until you're eighteen-years-old you have to be under the supervision of an adult. It's the law."

"Yeah, well, Pastor, I saw what the law did to my Pop. Shot him dead on our front porch," he replied staring out the window. "I don't think much of the law right now."

The pastor slowly pulled his car into the church parking lot and turned off the engine. "Penny, it's okay to be angry about what happened. It's okay to grieve about your father, but bitterness and un-forgiveness is not what he would have wanted from you right now."

Not wanting to hear any more discussion, Penny opened the car door and started walking to the pastor's house behind the church. Since the shooting, every adult he had contact with was telling him how he should feel, what he should do, and somehow knew what his father would say to him if he could. None of their advice would bring his pop back and hearing them talk about him just irritated him more. He could take care of himself and had done so since his mother died. As far as he was concerned they could all mind their own goddamned business.

The day of the shooting, the deputy sheriff in town had kept him in the second floor office of the courthouse for six hours asking him the same questions over and over again. He wanted to know how the sheriff got himself shot and what had happened to Dawes' revolver, saying that he could throw him in jail if he had taken the gun. Penny smiled as he remembered the look on the deputy's face when he had told him that if he had had the sheriff's pistol he'd of shot the son-of-a-bitch through the forehead the moment he'd driven in the yard.

"That's a hell of a thing to say, boy," the deputy had replied as he leaned back in his chair thinking that the kid was playing the hard case all the way.

"Yeah, well it wasn't your pop that got killed, was it?" Penny had announced angrily.

Later that evening, the pastor had picked him up with a stern warning from the deputy to keep an eye on the kid and that he might need to talk to him again if that revolver couldn't be found. He had informed him that he was not about to put up with any more bullshit, that the kid had taken that gun and he knew it. He just could not prove it... yet.

***

Penny quickly walked into the pastor's house to get the belongings that had been picked up from his house and checked the time on the big grandfather clock in the hallway. Five o'clock, plenty of time to get his things and head back out to the farm. It would be more than enough time to dig up the pistol and then get back to town in time to catch the westbound Acheson Topeka freight train that would be coming through at seven. For years he had heard it roll by the town in the dark. Tonight, he planned to be on it.

Once in his room, he dumped the sack of money on the bed and closed the door. He carefully counted eighty-eight dollars and twenty-four cents, a small fortune for a sixteen-year-old kid in 1939 Kansas.

There was a soft knock on the door. "Penny, are you all right?" It was the pastor's wife, a fat woman who always smiled and smelled like Ivory soap.

He quickly stuffed the money in his pockets. "Yes, ma'am. I'm fine."

"Okay, Hun. You need anything, you let me know. We'll be having supper in about an hour. Okay?" *Poor thing* she thought walking back to the kitchen, *probably in there crying his eyes out.* She would give him all the space and time he needed. She knew boys that age didn't like anyone seeing them crying.

As she sliced carrots and checked on the biscuits for dinner, she had no idea that Penny was already a quarter-mile away, running as fast as he could, having slipped out the bedroom window. By the time the pastor softly knocked on his door for dinner an hour later, Penny had already dug up the sheriff's pistol, repacked his small suitcase, and busted out every window of the only house he had ever lived in.

Before leaving the porch, he slowly knelt down and touched the large dried bloodstain where his father had died. "I love ya, Pop," he whispered. "I will never forget you." He kissed his fingertips and then touched the floor. High above, a solitary hawk drifted on the warm early evening wind that boiled up from the dusty fields below, a single witness to the start of something, an adventure born out of terrible hardship and loss, an adventure no one could have imagined. Penny Reynolds was on his way.

Chapter Two

For Brice Bailey this particular part of the country held a lot of bad memories. It also held more than a few law enforcement members that would like nothing better than to get their hands on him and stomp his balls to mush in some back-water holding cell. For the last three years he had been crisscrossing the country stealing everything that wasn't nailed down in every small town he landed in from Frisco to Detroit just to stay alive. *Man's gotta eat*, he would tell himself every time he pried off a lock or kicked in a door, an easy justification in these hard times. Depravation can make a man do things he would never normally do.

He had caught his first freight near the Atascadero Station on the California coast several years ago. He'd been a scared little killer on the run from the police for cooking the books in his favor to the tune of thirty-nine hundred dollars and then putting a paring knife through big Mike Lassiter's throat when he found out about it. One of the first investigators on the scene said he had never seen so much blood at a killing before. A week later the saturated hard wood office floor had to be ripped out and replaced just to get the smell out of the room.

For seven years Bailey had been the main bookkeeper at the Atlas Fruit Company in Atascadero, a thriving company in spite of the countrywide depression. Several days after big Mike's four-hundred-pound body had been found dead on the floor of his office, the embezzlement was discovered.

Bailey had been skimming cash for months in small amounts at first and then larger sums when the baby came and they moved into the new house on Camden Street. The auditors and the police soon connected the dots, and Bailey was about to be brought in for questioning. Knowing that the police were on the way, Bailey bid a tearful good-bye to his young wife and baby daughter and disappeared into the warm California night. That was three years ago, almost to the day.

The Atchison Topeka line started out in Kansas, rolled through Texas picking up baled cotton, Arizona - borax, and New Mexico -copper ingots before ending up in California where the flats would be loaded along with the boxcars and the run would be made back due east. Any Bo worth his salt knew all the spur lines along the way, knew when to get off, and knew when to get on. Since thirty-seven, the bulls, railroad agents who were nothing more than professional head knockers responsible for keeping riders off the trains, had been short-handed. Bailey knew this group well and went to great lengths to avoid them.

His railroad agent education had nearly cost him his life when he had been caught in the Abilene yard climbing down from an open boxcar just after midnight one night a year ago. He had waited in the dark on the roof as the first two men walked by. Confident they had moved on, he quickly climbed down the ladder and ended up literally in the middle of two more walking by. He never got a word out before the beating started. When it ended, he had lost both front teeth, suffered three broken ribs and had been kicked in the back and balls so hard that he pissed pink for a week. They had taken every nickel he had and then rolled his unconscious body down a steep ravine into the tall weeds at the far end of the yard. There were some people in this world you did not trifle with. Small town cops and railroad agents were some of those people.

Sitting in the open door of the boxcar as it slowly lumbered through town, Bailey lit the last of his hand-rolled cigarettes. He had been through Kansas before. Never had he seen a more depressing place in all his travels. The wind always blew, dropping a heavy dust on everything: people, cars, houses. Everything carried the same color, the same look of exhausted despair. Hell, when he thought about it, the whole goddamned country looked like that.

After smoking the butt down to his yellowed fingertips, he flicked the embers into the warm evening air just as some kid carrying a small suitcase sprinted from one of the buildings. To Bailey, the kid, looking to be maybe fifteen or sixteen, was running for all he was worth for the train. *Kid gonna get himself killed,* he thought, watching the boy get closer. He was now within reach of the open door of the car, stumbling and fighting to keep his footing on the heavy gravel.

Bailey stood leaning against the open door watching the kid run. "You're doing it wrong, dumbass!" he shouted. "Gonna get your legs chopped off."

The kid looked up, his face contorted with a mixture of fear and effort. "I need to get in!" he shouted. "Please, I need to get on."

Bailey knelt down as the train began to pick up speed. "You're gonna get killed trying to get on that way!" he yelled back.

"Please, mister, I gotta get on. Help me."

Bailey thought for a moment and then stood up. "Throw your case in here!" he shouted. The kid hesitated as the train picked up more speed. The boy was now running full out trying to keep up. "You're running out of time, kid. Throw it." In desperation Penny threw his suitcase into the darkened car. "All right!" shouted Bailey, "You gotta grab that ladder on the end. It's the only way."

With sweat streaming down his face and his heart feeling like it was about to pound out of his chest, Penny quickly spotted the heavy rung ladder bolted to the side of the car. With the last of his strength, he jumped as high on the rungs as he could. Every muscle in his arms and hands strained to hang on as he was jerked off his feet, his chest slamming into the bottom rung.

"Hang on, kid!" shouted Bailey laughing. "Pull yourself up. Go on, you can do it." He laughed as he watched the kid struggle up the ladder. *What a dumb ass,* he thought. If the kid fell, it would be good entertainment. He hadn't seen anybody fall off a moving train in some time. And whatever the boy was carrying in the case was just an added bonus.

He was already thinking about what he would do if the kid actually made it into the car. He looked fairly strong but shouldn't be too much trouble. Several minutes later Bailey watched as the kid carefully made his way around the sliding boxcar door and into the car. The two stood facing each other as the darkening Kansas landscape rolled by outside. "Goddamn, kid, didn't think you'd make it," announced Bailey smiling.

Still breathing heavy, Penny walked over and picked up his suitcase, keeping his eyes on the man. "Never caught a train before. Thanks for the help, though it wasn't much."

"Hell, youngster," shouted Bailey above the noise of the car, "I saved your goddamned life. If you had jumped on that open door, you'd a got sucked right under the wheels. Would of cut your dumb ass in half. The way I figure it, kid, you owe me."

"Mister, I don't want no trouble."

"Tell you what, boy, you give me that suitcase and we'll call it even. How's that? Besides, youngster, you're in my car. Everybody has to pay to ride."

"How bout I don't and you leave me alone!" shouted Penny backing up. He had seen this kind of man before - a no count drifter. One just like him had blown in on the wind last year and had knocked on the back door of their house asking for food. Penny's father had offered to let the man share a meal, but that would be the end of it. The man had seemed to take offense and pulled a short-bladed pocket knife, telling his father that he had better give him whatever money he had or he would get cut.

Penny remembered how his father, standing behind the screen door, had laughed at the threat and then in a flurry of heavy punches and kicks had beat three colors of shit out of the drifter. After dragging the unconscious intruder to the side of the road at the property line, Amon dropped a quarter on the man's chest, enough for a loaf of bread and a quart of milk, and walked away with a stern reminder not to start trouble with anymore hardscrabble Kansas dirt farmers. They never saw the man again.

"Never let a no count take anything from you," his father had announced at dinner that night. It had been the first he had spoken since the fight. "Never let a thief or a bully push you around. You understand? You stand up for what's right."

Penny stared at the knife in the man's hand. It was the first time in his life anyone had ever threatened him with a weapon. "I, ah, my Bible is in the case. I want to keep it," he replied trying to stay calm. "Like I said, mister, I don't want any trouble."

"Listen, you little peckerwood, trouble is here. Now get that Bible out and slide the case over here before I cut your goddamned ears off!" shouted Bailey. "You're on the hard road now, boy."

Penny slowly knelt down and opened the case. Bailey laughed as he folded his pocketknife and put it back in his pocket. Robbing the kid had been easy, hell, like taking candy from a baby. Hopefully the little punk had something of value in the suitcase. "You empty them pockets too, boy. I'll bet you got a dollar or two you stole from your momma's purse, you little shit." Walking over to pick up the case, he froze in mid-step as he saw the kid stand up with a pistol in his hand, the barrel looking as big as a canon. "Whoa, now goddamn it! You put that down before you shoot your toe off!" commanded Bailey, stepping back. Even in the muted light of the boxcar he could see the copper tips of the bullets in the revolver.

"You were gonna rob me!" shouted Penny, cocking the hammer. "You would leave me with nothing, you son of a bitch. All I wanted to do was get on the train and be left alone, and you were gonna take everything I had and probably try and kill me with that knife!" He was now screaming. "You don't know me, mister. You don't know me at all!"

Bailey stepped back farther into the car. If he could just get to the small axe he had next to his bedroll, he would be able to chop this crazy kid up. "Listen, boy, you need to calm down. Hell, I was just trying to scare ya. That's all. So why don't you put the gun down before somebody gets hurt. C'mon now."

Penny was having a hard time seeing the man as he stepped farther back into the shadows and a split second later he charged out of the darkness swinging a short handled axe. Bam! Bam! Terrified and strictly on reflex, Penny fired the .38 twice, tripping backwards over his suitcase, tumbling hard onto the rough wood floor.

In the space between the flash and bang of the pistol, Bailey honestly thought he could take the kid's head off with the axe. After all, he was a grown man, a seasoned Bo and this was just some half-starved peckerwood from nowhere Kansas. Stunned, he felt the first bullet hit him just below his bottom lip ripping through his jaw, shattering six teeth that came out in a spray just behind his right ear. He never felt the second one that punched through his heart and out his back. He was dead before he hit the floor.

Shocked by how fast everything had happened, Penny slowly got to his feet and stepped up close to the body of the man he had just killed. In the darkness, the spreading blood pool under the man's head looked black as ink. "I told you I didn't want no trouble, mister!" he shouted at the corpse. "You brought this on yourself, you son-of-a-bitch."

The gun smoke and smell of quick death hung heavy in the air as he drug the body by the arm to the door's edge, the dark Kansas landscape rushing by. With a final push, he rolled the dead man off the edge, the body tumbling disjointedly onto the ties and gravel below. He found the axe and tossed it out into the dark along with the man's bedroll and jacket. The only thing left to mark his presence was the blood on the floor and even that would be dry by sunrise.

Later that night Penny rolled into one of the dark corners of the car and fell into a deep exhausted sleep, a dreamless escape from the terrors of the day and the crushing pain of loneliness that was now setting in. Curled up in the dark, he let the clip clap sound of the wheels take him away, far away. Killing a man was hard work. He'd be in Colorado by morning.

"Hey, boy!" Penny turned to the voice. One of the two men he had seen getting off the train was walking up. "You need to watch your ass in this yard, kid," he said, walking by. "The goddamned bulls are everywhere." Penny could smell the man's sour sweat and chewing tobacco as he moved past. "They don't cotton to free riders and spuds like you."

Penny looked around nervously as the other man hurried by. "Hell, boy, you need to go home, back to your momma's tit," he said laughing.

Penny dropped his suitcase and stopped. His father wouldn't let another man talk to him that way, not ever. "Why don't you kiss my ass, mister," he shouted at the men.

Both stopped and turned as if they had heard the wooden ties start to sing. "What did you say, you little son-of-a-bitch?" questioned one of the men slowly walking back.

"You heard me, mister."

The man dropped his bedroll. "Tell you what, boy, I think I'm gonna bust you up just for the fun of it."

"C'mon, Jack, the kid ain't worth it!" shouted the other man. "Goddamned bulls are gonna show up any time. Then we got to fight them son's-a-bitches. Let's go. I need a beer."

Penny kept his right hand behind his back, tightly gripping the butt of the thirty-eight.

The man smiled without humor. "You're lucky, boy. I see your skinny ass again, I'm gonna cut your nuts off."

"We'll see!" shouted Penny as the man turned and hurried away. "I ain't afraid of a no-count like you."

As he watched the men disappear into a group of shanty buildings just past the rail yard, it was all he could do to keep his legs under him as he walked. He had been on the road just short of two days now and had already killed one man and had been threatened with dismemberment by another. Surely this was not going to be a daily occurrence? Hell, he thought stepping over the tracks, he only had four bullets left and California was still a long way off.

***

Kipper Moss took pride in his establishment, worked hard at keeping the place clean, made sure the beer was cold and the food hot, knowing full well that the hard men that filed in and out of his small café on a daily basis carried the open wounds of this new harsh reality. Most could pay for the short beers and coffee. For those who could not, he would direct them to a bench behind the building and at least make an attempt to help a fellow out. He wasn't running a charity house, but he recognized himself in the haggard faces of some of the men he saw, men who hadn't eaten in days, men who had worked all their lives and had lost everything but the clothes on their back and, now at their last stop, could not afford a nickel cup of coffee.

Kipper, a recent immigrant himself, knew poverty and depravation, had tasted it first hand in his native Germany several years earlier. Hitler had just come to power and with him had come an unsettling wave of ultra nationalism bordering on hysteria sweeping the country. Just before his father's death in thirty-five, the German Jews had been openly persecuted and victimized by the new government under Hitler. Beatings, arrests and property confiscation of Jewish assets had become a normal everyday occurrence throughout Germany by 1936. After SA Brown Shirts had destroyed his father's restaurant in Berlin twice in a year,

Kipper knew in his heart that as a Jew, if he had any hope for survival he would have to leave Germany. There was now nothing left for him in the only country he had ever known. His mother had died years before his father, and being an only child, he had run the business by himself up until the day he burned the place to the ground and two days later boarded a ship out of Dresden.

His timing in coming to the United States in hopes of rebuilding a dream economically could not have been worse. He had processed through Ellis Island, April 23,1937, a day of exhaustive joy and heavy melancholy - joy at being able to build a new life without fear, deep sadness at the fact that he would be doing it alone. The golden shore country his father had often talked about was now in the grip of the Depression. A grinding wave of economic poverty and solid despair had hit hard, leaving the American population dazed and desperate.

After two weeks in the city of New York, he knew he would have to go west, far away from the soup kitchens, the bread lines, and the massive lack of opportunity. As an immigrant, starting a new business on the thoroughly burnt over ground of the city was untenable. Over the next year he taught himself English by reading newspapers and moved west with the growing tide of men, all looking for a new start, a new life. To stay alive he cut timber for a dollar a day in West Virginia, picked fruit in Florida for a nickel a basket, and dug for opals in Arkansas, all the while keeping the fifty gold coins he had brought from Germany safe. Fortunately, had sewn the coins into the lining of his heavy coat. Even after being beaten and left for dead in the stockyards of Abilene, Kansas, just before Christmas, the coins had remained safe.

The following summer he arrived in Big Spring, Colorado, and knew the minute he jumped down from the freight car that this would be where he would attempt the dream. After a short negotiation, he bought the closed and dilapidated café from old man Douglas, put every cent he had into it, and now, a full two years from first stepping foot in the country, he was the proud owner of the new *Whistle Stop Café and Bar*, the one business in town that was doing almost as well as all four of the whore houses combined.

Much to his surprise, he had found it easy to make deals with the various railroad men who were more than eager to pick up food supplies along the route, taking their cut on the back end from the café's booming business. Everything from Kansas beef and pork to fish and seafood from the coast found their way into the kitchen of the Whistle Stop. The word soon spread that the best steak in the West was grilled and served at the Whistle Stop.

Kipper noticed the kid the moment he stepped through the door. A tall, skinny, dark haired boy not more then sixteen, carrying a small battered suitcase tentatively walked in and sat down on one of the counter stools. To Kipper, he could not remember a face being more out of place in the crowded room. The kid looked as if he were just off the farm, a frail animal about to be devoured by the loud tough crowd of hard men all around him.

"Hello, young man," announced Kipper, stepping up on the other side of the counter. "What can I do for you?"

Penny nodded and leaned forward, the din of the room nearly drowning out his voice, "Do you have hamburgers?"

"Of course. Is that what you want to order?"

"Yes, sir. I want two of them with extra onions and two root beers."

Kipper smiled and leaned across the counter. "No offense, my young friend, but that's going to cost eighty-five cents. You got that kind of weight?"

Penny thought for a moment and then pulled a crumpled one-dollar bill from his pocket and dropped it on the counter. "That should cover it," he replied solemnly. It was only the second time in his life he had ordered a hamburger or any food for that matter. The first time had been at the Kansas State Fair three years ago. His father had taken him along and they had bought hamburgers from a small stand and drank Hires Root Beer. For Penny, it had been one of the best days of his life, one of the few happy times he could remember.

"Yep, that will cover it, my young friend," replied Kipper picking up the bill. "Two hamburgers with extra onions coming up." As he put the bill in the register, he knew the youngster was now in real trouble. A half-dozen of the men sitting in the café were now paying quiet attention to the kid, watching his every move. Young ones, especially one this scrawny, didn't ride the hard road, and if they did, they didn't have enough walking around money to buy food in a café full of down-on-your-luck drifters and others who'd just as soon cut your throat for a dime as look at you. No, the boy was in deep and didn't even know it.

Kipper knew that if he didn't do something in the kid's favor pretty quickly, his body would be found the next day. Trying to think of what he should do, he fried up the burgers, poured the root beers, and set the fare on the counter in front of the kid. "You need anything else, young man, just holler. Okay?"

Penny nodded and then quickly started eating the food, ignoring the attention he had drawn. He had seen the stares when he walked in, heard the whispers but right now all he cared about was the hot food in front of him. If anyone in the room wanted to start anything, he had four bullets left in the .38 tucked in the belt under his coat. He had used it once and would damn sure use it again if anyone pushed the issue.

"Whoa, slow down, my friend," announced Kipper smiling, watching the kid eat. "You'll bite off your fingers eating that fast."

Penny looked up from his plate. "You my mother?" he replied, his mouth full.

Kipper leaned across the counter. "No, I am not your dear mother, my tough young friend, but if she were here, she would tell you the same thing."

Penny looked around the room now noticing that several of the men were watching him closely.

Kipper leaned across the counter. "Tell you what, why don't you bring your food around to the back part of the kitchen. There's a small table back by the sink. Not so many prying eyes."

Penny took another quick bite of the burger. "You think they'll be trouble?" he asked, his mouth full.

Kipper looked around the room and nodded. "Pretty much guarantee it, my friend. C'mon. Bring your food." Penny thought for a moment and then picked up his small suitcase and plate, following the big German towards the kitchen.

Once in the back, Kipper pointed to the small makeshift table by the sink. "You can sit over there. Nobody will bother you." The short fat cook nodded and then went back to his grill. Penny pulled up the single chair and continued to eat. Kipper walked over and set his drinks down. "Here 'ya go. If you need anything else, just let me know."

"I need my change," replied Penny through a mouthful of burger. "You owe me fifteen cents."

Kipper smiled, "Right you are, sir. Here you go." He dug three nickels out of his grease-stained apron and set them on the table. Penny nodded, quickly scooped up the coins, and shoved them in his pocket.

"So where you plan on staying while you're here in our fair town?" questioned Kipper.

Penny looked over his shoulder, then back to his food. "Don't look too fair to me," he replied taking another big mouthful.

"Well, you can't judge a book by its cover, my young friend. There are some decent people here. We have a couple of school teachers, two lawyers, and even a mayor."

Penny continued to eat, wondering why the big man with the strange accent was still talking to him. To Penny, the man looked like he was probably born sweating, with his short red hair plastered to his head and the sweat running down the side of his face. Although it was hot in the cafe, he didn't think it was that hot. He told a long drink of his root beer thinking the man might have some kind of illness. Probably caught it wherever he was from.

"So, have you thought about where you're staying?" asked Kipper picking up Penny's empty plate.

"There's a hotel down the street; costs five dollars for a bed and bath."

Penny set his root beer down. "Five dollars just to sleep?"

Kipper laughed. "Yes, sir, and that's the cheapest. The other two hotels run eight and ten dollars a night."

Penny shook his head, swallowed the last of his drink and stood up. "Thank you for the table. I'm gonna head out now."

Watching the boy pick up his suitcase and head out the back screen door, Kipper could not shake the feeling that he had to do something for the kid. It was already dark outside and the human predators would be out. Big Spring was a tough town after sunset. The kid would be no match.

"Hey," announced Kipper following Penny outside.

"My house is just up the hill, right up there. There's a cot on the back porch. It's safe, and I'll give you a blanket after I close up. It's a lot better than sleeping in the weeds down by the tracks."

Penny thought for a moment, "Why you doing this, mister? You don't know me."

"You got enemies here, lad, men who would kill you for what you got in your pockets." Kipper stepped out into the dark feeling the cool night air wash over him. "Look, I don't want anything from you. It's just that I really don't think this place is safe for a kid to wander around in at night. Take the cot."

Still not sure why this big red-headed stranger wanted to help him, a dry cot on a dry porch did sound a whole lot better than walking back down to the rail yard to sleep in the weeds. Besides, he still had his pistol, and if the big foreigner tried to rob him during the night, he would shoot him dead without a second thought.

"Okay, mister. I'll take the porch. Thank you." He turned and started walking up the slope.

"Say, young fella, what's your name?" asked Kipper.

Penny turned around in the dark. "Name's Penny, Penny Reynolds. Thanks again for the cot, mister."

"Okay, my name's Kipper. I'll drop that blanket off later." He waited for the kid to answer but no reply came. The only sound was the hush, huff and whistle of the six-0-one freight pulling out of the yard headed for Denver.

Chapter Four

From where he lay on the rickety cot on Kipper's back porch, Penny watched the sunrise turn from deep purple, to red, to a bright orange as it crested in a brilliant spray over the Rockies. It had been well after midnight when he felt someone drop the heavy purple and white quilt over him as he dozed. The night had been cold and the blanket had been a welcomed friend.

"Aye, you're awake," announced Kipper from behind the screen door. "Are you hungry? I have to go open up."

Penny threw back the blanket and sat up. "How much is breakfast?" he asked pulling on his shoes.

Kipper laughed, stepping out on the porch. "No charge, sir. Besides, I need to pay you for guarding my porch."

Penny stood up stamping his feet, the cold morning air sending a shiver down his back. "What do you mean?"

Kipper pointed to the cot. "Don't forget your gun. I just assumed you were guarding the place."

Penny looked down and spotted the pistol on the cot. It had fallen out of his waistband during the night. Not knowing what else to do, he quickly picked it up and stuck it in his back belt line.

"You know, you need to be careful with that. Many a gunman has shot his own toes off," announced Kipper lighting his pipe.

Penny pulled on his coat. "I know how to handle the gun," he said, locking eyes with the German. "It's mine."

Kipper smiled holding up both hands. "Not a problem, Penny. It's your gun. Just mind your fingers and toes. C'mon, breakfast is on me. Leave your suitcase just inside the door of the house. Nobody will bother it."

Penny thought for a moment and then set the case inside. "I can pay for my food," he replied following Kipper down the porch steps. "Don't need no charity."

"Tell ya what," announced Kipper as he continued walking down the slope, "Don't think of it as charity. Think of it as someone just being friendly. But if you still feel bad, send me a dollar when you get on your feet. How would that be?"

"That's fine," replied Penny. "I'll keep a sum. I pay my way."

Later that morning, Kipper fixed them both a full breakfast of eggs, toasts, and sausage. Each sat and ate, enjoying the quiet yet growing bond between them. For Kipper, he could see the distant image of himself in the skinny kid with sad eyes. The tough exterior hid a pain or wound that would crust over with time but would never heal. It was the universal injury of loss.

By nine o'clock, Kipper had unlocked the front doors of the café allowing a steady stream of cold, hungry men inside. To Penny, it was hard distinguishing one from the other. They all carried the same beat-down look of men who had gone without the softness of life for far too long. Their clothes smelled of campfires and chewing tobacco and their communications were little more than mumbled words and subtle nods. The hard road took a toll, numbing the spirit while beating the body. Penny knew he was lucky to have the cot on the back of Kipper's porch, knowing that many men his father's age had slept in the tall wet grass along the tracks, men who wrapped themselves in dirty blankets and faded memories of friends, family, and much better times.

By nine-thirty, the cook showed up smelling of sweat and gin but had soon begun to roll out the steady stream of fried eggs, hash browns, and meat for the crowd inside. Penny sat at the small table by the sink in the back drinking his third cup of coffee, watching the constant stream of men coming and going from the café. It was amazing how many people shuffled in and had breakfast. Even several ladies from the whorehouse across the street came in and ate, their presence barely noticed by the men inside.

"You know, Penny, if you had a mind of staying awhile, I could use a hand here," announced Kipper, stacking an armful of dirty plates and saucers in the large metal sink. "I could pay you a fair wage."

Penny thought for a moment. He really didn't have any place to go and getting there in a hurry really didn't make sense when he thought about it. "How come you're offering me the job?" he asked.

Kipper took the hand towel off his shoulder and wiped the sweat off his face. "I know how you feel, you know, not being with your family and all. Thought maybe I could help. Besides, my busser ran off two days ago."

Penny let the memory of his mother in her faded blue dress on the front porch in Kansas flash and then fade. The mind's eye picture of her brought more pain than he had expected. "Well, I guess I can stay awhile. What kind of job are you talking about?"

Kipper smiled. "You can clear the tables and wash the dishes. I'll pay you two dollars a day and take care of feeding ya and putting a roof over your head while you're here. How does that sound?"

Penny stood up and shook Kipper's hand in disbelief. *God almighty*, he thought, *two dollars a day just for washing dishes?* "Sounds like a good deal to me." For a sixteen-year-old in 1939, it was a king's ransom. Any man in the room would have jumped at the chance to work for a third of those wages.

"Good," replied Kipper smiling. He pulled a clean white apron out from under the counter. "You can start now. The lunch crowd will be here before you know it."

***

A hundred miles due east, past the dusty scrub flats of mesquite brush and broken bluffs, Inspector Dane Palmer rolled the bloated body onto its back, releasing a small flurry of blow flies. The other railroad agent stepped back holding his nose. "Goddamn, there's a ripe one."

Palmer knelt down next to the corpse studying the bloody and blackened face. "This man's been shot, AW. Look here." He picked up a small twig and slowly pushed it into the blood crusted hole just under the man's left eye."

"Jesus," whispered the other agent still holding his nose. "That's a hard thing you just did."

Palmer stood up pulling the stick out of the wound. "Hell, AW, he ain't feeling a thing. Looks like whoever blew that tunnel through his head did so a couple days ago."

AW spit tobacco, wiping his chin. "So what do you want to do?"

Palmer took off his hat with a sigh, looking around the desolate landscape. "Well, this one is ours. That tub of guts sheriff ain't gonna be of any help to a couple cinder dicks. I can guarantee you that. He ain't got out of the car since we got here."

AW spit again. "Never liked those Mingo County boys; bunch of assholes."

Palmer knelt down again next to the body and reached into the dead man's back pocket. "Got a billfold here, pard. Let's see. I'll be damned. Got six, seven dollars," he announced stuffing the bills into his own pocket.

"Hey, I get half," demanded AW stepping forward.

"The hell you do; I'm the one who stuck my hand in bloody shit to get the wallet. So back off. Besides, I have seniority."

"Christ almighty, Dane, you got on with the railroad two weeks before I did. That don't make you senior by much."

Palmer looked up and then back to the wallet smiling, "Well, AW, it's enough time for that money to stay in my pocket. Now, you want to keep pushing the debate or you want to help me find out who shot this sorry son-of-a-bitch?"

"Well, if you ain't gonna give me any of that money, then, by God, you're buying lunch."

Palmer nodded looking back at the body. "Fair enough, AW. Why don't you see if there's a blanket or something in the car to wrap this guy up in,"

AW looked back at the fat sheriff dozing behind the wheel of the car. "How the hell we gonna get the body back to town?"

Palmer nudged the dead man's leg with the toe of his boot. "Well, he's a bit stiff but I guess he's soft enough to fold him in the trunk."

AW laughed. "The sheriff ain't gonna like a shit-smelling dead man shoved in his trunk."

"Yeah, well I quit thinking about what that sheriff thinks about an hour ago," replied Palmer lighting a cigarette. "Go on. See if he's got a blanket or a tarp. It's hot out here and I need a beer."

As AW walked off chuckling to himself, Palmer stood, looking up into the late afternoon sun. For a moment he thought about drawing his pistol and taking a shot at the two large turkey buzzards that were circling silently high overhead. *Hell,* he thought flicking his cigarette butt at the body, *I ought to just walk away and let the buzzards do their job. Wouldn't take more than a week for them to pick him down to nothing.*

Finding dead drifters on railroad property had become routine, discoveries that were now costing the company real money. By law, any fatality that occurred within ten feet of either side of the track or gravel bed was the Railroad's responsibility. Local law enforcement was more than happy to let the train investigators foot the bill for recovery and subsequent burial of all the bodies.

Intuitively, Palmer knew that no matter how many dead men he found or bums he threw off the main line, he would never reach the rarefied air where railroad senior management existed, a place he really wanted to go. In these hard times, any kind of progression through the ranks of any business was nearly impossible. If you did not have the connections, which he did not, you stayed in your box and thanked God Almighty, Himself every night that you even had one to begin with. He knew he was nothing more than a thumb breaker with a badge, one of the guys who shoveled the discarded piles of human refuse every day and thanked his betters with a smile for the opportunity to do so. Out on the main line, he was just another one of the enforcers, a small time player, a nobody in a world of broken men.

Yeah, the buzzards would do a better job than I could ever do, he thought watching AW walk back from the sheriff's car with a dirty blue blanket. *Far better.*

Chapter Five

It had been four days since he had arrived in Big Spring and he was beginning to settle into a comforting rhythm of bussing tables, emptying the trash, and washing the endless stream of dishes. It wasn't hard work. In fact, he kind of liked the hustle and bustle of the café and the endless conversations he had with Kipper about his life in Germany.

He liked the fact that Kipper did not pry into his own life in Kansas but kept a respectful distance from the subject. He was still sleeping on the German's porch, having declined an offer to stay in Kippers' spare bedroom. He still did not feel right about moving into the house but instead settled for an extra blanket and a hot shower, comforts that more than made up for not sleeping inside four walls. Kipper had kept his word about the wages, giving him two dollars every evening when the café closed.

It was late on the afternoon of the fifth day from his arrival when Kipper walked into the restaurant kitchen visibly upset. Penny was washing the last bit of plates and cups at the sink as Kipper sat down at the small table reading a German newspaper. "Madness!" he shouted, slamming the paper down. "This, this lunatic has invaded Poland. I have friends who live there. He is going to start a world war. We will all suffer," he announced pointing a finger at Penny.

Penny had never seen the German so worked up. "Who is going to cause a war?" he asked, drying a plate.

Kipper shook his head. "My God, you Americans have no idea how dangerous Hitler really is. Mark my words, he will cause millions of people to die."

"What is he, some kind of president or something?" asked Penny stacking the plates on the shelf.

Kipper got up from the table and tossed the paper in the trashcan by the door. "He is the Devil, my young friend," he replied sadly. "Soon he will be known by everyone."

Penny wanted to ask more questions but thought better of it as Kipper slammed the back screen door open and walked into the dark behind the café. He remembered seeing his father on several occasions this upset and knew then, as he did now, to stay clear.

***

Eighty miles to the east and headed to Big Spring at fifty miles an hour, railroad agents Dane Palmer and AW Moss sat in the dining car eating an early supper. It had been three days since they had talked to the Colorado Springs Medical Examiner about the dead man they had found on the tracks.

The ME, a testy old son-of-a-bitch in Palmer's mind, had a personality that was downright irritating. In the morgue, Palmer had asked if there were any other details concerning the death of the man, and the ME had looked over the top of his glasses and said, "Other than being shot twice, what do you want to know?"

"I don't know, doc, maybe you were able to dig a bullet out?"

"Nope, both went clear through."

"Any other signs of a struggle on the body?"

"Wasn't looking."

Palmer had thought for a moment. "You know, you're not giving me much to go on. I'm trying to figure out who did this. It's my job."

The ME had chuckled. "Your job? Well, if you did not notice, I am backed up in here till hell freezes over. I don't have time to waste talking about how some hard-road-bum got himself killed. I got three more in the cooler from the PD that I need to attend to." He had handed the file across the desk. "Here's my report. What I can tell you is that our man was shot at close range, looks like a .38 by the holes. Whoever shot him was either sitting down when he fired or is a shorty. The bullets hit in an upward angle. So go find a short bum with a thirty-eight."

Palmer had taken the file and handed it to AW. "That's it? You trying to be funny?"

"That's it. And I quit trying to be funny years ago. Now, if you'll excuse me, I have work to do. I'm sure you can find your way out."

Now, a day later, Palmer drank down the last of his beer in the dining car, watching AW woof down his food. The man had the worst table manners he had ever seen. "Jesus, how do you keep from choking to death eating like that?"

AW looked up in surprise, his mouth full. "What?"

"You eat like you're starving."

AW went back to his plate without answering. He didn't particularly like Palmer but knew he had a reputation for solving cases. Being attached to a winner in these hard times was always a good thing. Besides, if he got too pushy or aggravating, agents fell off trains and died every day. One more wouldn't make a goddamn bit of difference. He'd let Palmer play the big shot but only for so long. "So why we headed to Big Spring?" he asked, washing down a mouthful of food with the warm beer. He belched before Palmer could answer.

Palmer shook his head while lighting a cigarette. "That's the nearest town on this part of the line. It's as good a place as any to look around and start asking questions."

AW laughed. "Short guy with a thirty-eight. Shit this should be easy."

Palmer blew a lung full of smoke to the ceiling. "Yeah, well that's all we got. You have a better idea on what we should do, I'm all ears."

AW sat back and belched again. The sound caught the attention of an older woman sitting by herself two tables down. A quick look of disdain crossed between them. AW winked at the woman and then nodded to Palmer, smiling, "Older women love me. They really do."

Palmer looked back at the woman who had to be in her seventies. "Yeah, looks about your speed. You ought to bring her back to the sleeper tonight. She might be a hell cat."

AW laughed and thumped the table. "Hell, if we weren't working, I probably would; the older the violin - the sweeter the music."

Palmer shook his head while pulling out his pocket watch, not wanting to prolong the conversation any longer about the woman. "It's five-thirty. We got about forty-five minutes till we get in to Big Spring." He stood up and pulled a toothpick out of the small table dispenser. "I gotta take a shit. See ya back at the sleeper."

He walked off, nodding to the old woman as he passed her table. Up close she looked a lot older than seventy. He pushed open the dining car door and stepped out onto the steel grate platform, adjusting the holster on his belt under his coat and breathing in the cool early evening air. Even though he would never admit that AW was right, the chances of finding the killer anywhere along the line was a high stakes' gamble at best. He flicked his cigarette butt onto the blur of ties below. Hell, a third of the male population in the country was now riding the hard road. Finding one asshole with a gun was a needle in a haystack.

As he looked out onto the wide-open landscape, a nearly overpowering feeling of melancholy swept over him. In his mind, in the grand scheme of things who really gave a red piss who killed the drifter, a nobody shot dead by another nobody in a sea of no-counts and malcontents. Before stepping across the platform between the cars, he shook the sadness off remembering that compared to most of the working population, he had it pretty good. Four hundred dollars a month was a lot of money and he did have the authority to do pretty much whatever he wanted to do as long as he carried a railroad investigator's badge.

Palmer smiled while stepping into the next car on his way to the bathroom. If he remembered right, Big Spring had a couple of fairly decent whorehouses, places that almost made the trip worthwhile. A good five-dollar ride might be just the thing he needed. After that he would ask a few questions, make a few notes, write his report, and head back to Kansas. His girlfriend would be glad to see him, and he truly did miss her soft round bottom and good cooking. *Yeah*, he thought, *I have it pretty good.*

Chapter Six

Penny was on the back porch of the café eating the last of his supper when he heard the whistle of the six o'clock train from Colorado Springs roll into the station. Kipper had calmed down a bit from the newspaper article and was now loudly talking politics with the cook, a quiet drifter with a huge western moustache who carried an air of tired indifference about life but knew how to cook. As Kipper had said several times, the key to the café's success was Earle behind the grill.

In reality Earle Caswell, café cook, was really Earle Caswell, inmate #854197 from the Deer Lodge Montana State prison, having completed a nine-year stretch for beating to death a stockbroker from Butte during a drunken brawl. He had done his time, kept his nose clean and drifted into Big Spring like a thousand other guys looking for a place to stick. He had learned to cook in prison, had become so good at the culinary arts that it was rumored the warden kept extending his sentence just to keep him in the prison kitchen.

When he first came to town two years ago, he had walked into Kipper's café and stayed for three hours nursing two cups of coffee and a slice of pie, all the while watching the cook struggle to get all the orders out for the growing crowd of hungry men. Earle had been able to tell that the cook had done little to no kitchen prep the night before in order to handle the lunch and dinner service today. In his years in Deer Lodge he had prepared thousands of meals for the inmates, learning the lesson early on that in order to feed large groups of men, kitchen prep for meat and vegetables and sauces had to be done in advance, sometimes days in advance. He had stayed till closing time and then made his pitch about how he could do a better job and that the food he fixed would be the best any of the men who were on the hard road would ever eat.

Kipper had seemed impressed and asked him where he had received such a high level of culinary ability. He had thought for a moment, knowing full well that he would not get a second chance to tell the truth. He had taken a deep breath, looked Kipper in the eye and said, "Montana State penitentiary in Deer Lodge. Did a seven-year stretch for manslaughter."

He remembered the fleeting look of apprehension that clouded Kipper's face as he digested the information. After a moment of reflection he had spoken up. "You sorry you did it?"

Earle had shaken his head slowly. "More than you know, sir. A big piece of me died that night. Been a hard seven years," he had replied, his voice barely a whisper. Kipper had seen the same look of loss and pain in his father's eyes the second time the Brown Shirts had broken all the windows and severely vandalized the candy shop. He had hired Earle on the spot, not really sure of his reason. It had proven to be one of the best business decisions he ever made.

Kipper was just about to close up when Palmer and AW walked up on the porch and knocked on the café window. "Hey, Mister, can I talk to you a minute?" asked Palmer through the glass.

"We're closed!" shouted Kipper from behind the counter inside.

Palmer took his badge out of his pocket and pressed it against the window. "Won't take but a minute."

Kipper took off his apron and walked over to the front door, unlocking the dead bolt. "What's the trouble, officer?" he asked stepping out onto the porch.

Palmer lit a cigarette. "Mind if we step inside? Need to ask you a few questions."

Whether they were Gestapo, State Police, or local law enforcement, to Kipper they all exhibited the same type of body language, a posture of defense, a guarded stance that announced fear and aggression, both at the same time. To anyone who had been exposed to men like this, the demeanor was easily identified. Police were police, no matter what country they were from.

Kipper stepped farther out onto the porch, closing the door behind him. "What's this about?" he asked, studying the faces of the men.

Palmer flicked the butt into the street. "Are you the owner?"

"Yes, this is my place."

Palmer looked into the window. "Looks like you're closing up. Any chance we can still get a cup of coffee? I promise we won't be long."

Kipper thought for a moment as a cool gust of evening wind blew past the porch. "Okay, sure. C'mon in."

***

Later that night, just before Penny rolled into his blankets, Kipper slowly walked out of the dark and stepped up onto his back porch. He pulled up one of the chairs by the back door and sat down with a sigh, his breath a small frosty cloud. "I had some interesting visitors tonight," he announced from the dark.

"Yeah, who's that?" asked Penny, pulling off his boots and setting them under the bunk.

"Two railroad detectives."

A sudden shiver ran down Penny's back, a response that had nothing to do with the chill in the air. "Ah, what did they want with you?"

"Nothing with me. Said they were looking for someone who had killed some Bo on the train. They asked me if I had seen anyone with a pistol, maybe someone who had passed through here in the last week or so."

Penny stared at Kipper's barely visible shape in the dark. "What did you tell em?"

Penny watched as Kipper lit his pipe, the orange light of the match illuminating his face. "I told them that I hadn't seen any 'man' with a gun - not a lie. Now, if they had asked me if I had seen a skinny young boy with a pistol, my answer might have been different."

Penny reached back under the bed and began pulling on his boots. "What are you trying to say?" The fragile emotional framework of stability and security he had started to build in his heart over the past week was beginning to collapse.

"Penny, did you kill that man?" asked Kipper softly. "Did you shoot someone with that pistol I saw?" He already knew the answer, the question hanging heavy in the air like a bad smell.

After a moment, Penny stood up and pulled on his coat. "Sure did. He was going to chop me up with an axe so I shot him. And I would do it again. The son-of-a-bitch had it coming."

"My God," whispered Kipper from the dark. "Do you realize what you have done?"

"God had nothing to do with what I done," announced Penny stuffing his two clean shirts and extra pair of socks in his small suitcase. "If you don't mind, Kipper, can you give me an hour before you tell them fellas who I am?"

"Sit down, Penny," announced Kipper. "I'm not telling the police anything but I need you to tell me everything that happened. I have to know."

"Yeah? And why is that? What if I don't want to talk about it? You don't know me. You don't know where I've been."

Kipper thought for a moment. He really didn't have the right or the influence to ask the hard questions. The kid with the hard eyes was a stranger, like a wounded wild animal that showed up on his doorstep in the middle the night too injured and too exhausted to go anywhere else. "You're right, Penny. I have no idea what you have seen or where you have been. But what I do know is that a sixteen-year-old boy should never have to carry the burden you are carrying."

Penny picked up his suitcase and stepped off the porch while buttoning his coat. "I'm much obliged, Kipper, for the hospitality and the job but I'm gonna hit the road now."

"Listen to me, Penny. We can make this right. We can tell the authorities your side of the story. C'mon stay. Let me help you get through this trouble."

Penny turned and looked back at the porch. "Sorry, Kipper, I saw what the law did to my pa. Took everything we had, and, when we had nothing left, they took his life. I don't have nothing to say to those people, and I damn sure don't trust em."

"Penny, come on back," called Kipper watching him fade into the darkness. "Penny, it doesn't have to be this way. Penny."

For a moment he thought about running after the kid, getting him by the scruff of his neck and shaking some sense into him, but then again what responsibility did he really have here? He had only known the boy a week, hardly time enough to get a clear picture of anyone's character. Feeling the cold night close in around him, he sat back in his chair feeling a deep sense of loss and emotional failure. God, fate, or whatever power controlled the lives of men had brought this troubled boy into his world, and for all his charity, he could do nothing to stop the bleeding. He sat on the porch well into the night, watching the darkness and the cold white sparkle of stars overhead. The kid was gone.

Chapter Seven

It had been six days since he walked off of Kipper Moss's porch in Big Spring, been six days and five nights of hitchhiking on Route 60 north bound. As he walked along the road, memories of his mother and father would come back in a rush, pastel pictures of supper together and fragments of laughter - soft days before the sickness came. He had watched his father change from the worry, physically bent under the weight of what was to come. The quick smile that had been so much a part of his personality had slowly disappeared, replaced by a silent heaviness that seemed to cover him like a shroud. If he slept three hours a night, it had been rare. His mother's cough and horrific struggle to breathe had kept him by her side night and day. The dust had taken her life away one hacking cough at a time, and there wasn't a thing anyone could have done about it.

Kicking an empty peaches can into the ditch as he walked, the memory of watching his dad washing his mother's bed clothes brought a jolt of physical pain to his heart. In her coughing fits she had frequently soiled herself, an embarrassment that had troubled her deeply. His father had held her close and reassured her in quiet whispers that it was nothing and that he would take care of it. Everyday Penny had watched him change the linens and do the wash, a labor of love from a man who would have done anything to make her feel better, anything.

As the days of slowly watching his mother die had turned into weeks, something hard and sharp had begun to grow inside him. A deep-seated anger had taken root, a barely controlled rage at the crushing unfairness of it all. His father had worked himself to the bone trying to give them the things they would never really have. The land always took more than it gave and now the dust had been taking the one true treasure his father ever had. After she died that warm day in May, most of what would pass for life in his father died with her.

Penny remembered that his father hadn't cried at the funeral. By the time she had mercifully drifted away, all his tears had been used up. All he had had left was a handful of dirt he dropped on her coffin. A year and four days after they lowered her into the ground, the sheriff had shown up at the farm and finished the job the dust had started. The dust had taken it all.

For several nights after leaving Big Spring, Penny slept in the woods, doing the best he could to fight off the cold and bugs. He had already spent five dollars on food from one of the small markets on the road. He wanted to save money, but on the third day, his feet sore from walking, covered in dirt and road grime, he gave himself a treat and checked into a small motor lodge right on the Idaho/Montana border, having been dropped off by a passing logging crew truck on its way up to Missoula.

The old lady never even batted an eye when he checked in. Didn't seem at all surprised that a skinny kid had come in off the highway and paid the six dollars cash for a two-night stay. She took the money, dropped it in a cigar box, and slid a key across the counter. "Cabin number four," she announced pointing out the window. "And don't steal nothing."

Penny nodded. "Yes, ma'am. Ah, where can I get something to eat? I can pay."

The old woman leaned on the counter her watery pale blue eyes sizing him up. "Where's your kin, boy? Don't see many young'uns coming through here by themselves."

To Penny, her inquiry carried a sharp edge, an edge that immediately made him wary of how he should answer. "Kin's in Montana. I'm headed up to see em." It was a lie of course. But the more he talked to the old woman, the more ill at ease he became. He could not shake the notion that this lady did not have his best interests at heart. For a second he thought about asking for his money back but then checked the thought, remembering that he still had four bullets in the pistol, more than enough to take care of any trouble she might decide to send his way.

"There's a store just down the road," she said finally. "They got potted meat, bread, and such, not a lot, but by the look of ya, I doubt you eat much."

Penny smiled. "Yes, ma'am, that will be fine." He turned and left the office, not wanting to continue the conversation any longer than he had to. Outside, the air carried a cold bite and a grey overcast that announced snow. He walked across the lodge's wide gravel lot and back to the road, pulling his coat collar tight, still not having any real plan about his future other than to keep moving. Looking west he could see the small red and white general store sign a hundred yards farther up the road.

As he walked, he did a quick calculation on how much money he had left. He had just spent six dollars on the cabin and taking into account the three dollars he had spent on food the last two days, he figured he had seventy-eight dollars left. Damn, he thought, this was only the fourth day since leaving Kipper's place, and he had already spent close to ten dollars. And that wasn't even counting the food he was about to buy today. Son-of-a-bitch, he thought, at this rate he would be out of money in a week.

He brushed back a tear as an overwhelming sadness washed over him. He would give anything to have someone tell him it was going to be okay, someone to give him just a small word of encouragement. He had never missed his parents more than he did at that moment. For him, the world had suddenly become a very large, lonely place. For a second he thought about going back to Kipper's place, back to the cot on the porch, back to the one person in the world who cared about him.

He stepped off the road as a heavy lumber truck fully loaded with logs rumbled up behind him and then roared past, throwing a fine silt into the air. Just as he wiped the grit from his eyes that had stuck to his tears, a strange yet oddly familiar smell of burnt stone filled the air. A heartbeat later, a jagged thirty-five-mile long lightning bolt flashed out of the grey overcast sky, slamming into the top of a seventy-foot blue spruce only yards away from where he stood. The thunderclap bolt exploded the tree into a shower of white-hot embers, the shock wave violent enough to knock him off his feet and into the ditch on the other side of the road.

Lying face down in the tall grass unable to move, he watched a small beetle slowly walk across the back of his hand and then disappear into the weeds. There was no sound, just a dull constant tone, like a bell ringing under water. He could taste blood. Still unable to move, he ran his tongue over his teeth and discovered several jagged edges on the right side. Slowly, with a grunting effort, he began to move his fingers, then his hands, and then, after what seemed like an hour of work, was able to push himself to his knees. In all of his sixteen and a half years on the planet he had never felt this kind of pain - a raw agony that radiated from the top of his head to the bottom of his feet. It even hurt to blink. Still confused as to what had just happened, he slowly stood and discovered that he was no longer wearing shoes and only had on one sock.

As his mind began to clear a bit, he looked across the road, stunned to see that almost the entire side of the road he had been walking on was now on fire, the heat from the four-foot flames radiating across the pavement. He stumbled back into the grass looking for his shoes and suitcase. It hurt to walk. His knees seemed to lock up and then release, his muscles reacting seconds after the effort. The smoke from the growing fire was now making it hard to breathe and see as he continued to look for his shoes and suitcase in the tall deer grass. "Son-of-a-bitch!" he shouted in frustration, the smoke and heat growing more intense. Now beginning to choke and spit, he broke into a disjointed trot down the ditch, the flames getting higher by the second.

The snap and pop of the blaze and the sound of his labored breathing filled his ears as he continued to run through the knee high grass, his legs still numb and disjointed. His vision began to narrow as the fear of dying slowly eased. He knew he was not going to make it, and strangely, the resignation of his fate settled gently, slowing his run to a walk. He was dying and for a blessed moment he saw his father standing in front of him, his hand out-stretched, a smile of deep contentment radiating from his face. Penny took a final step for the hand and then fell into a soft blackness that pulled him deep. He had never felt such peace, such comfort. His last fleeting thought was *this is what it feels like to die -glorious.*

Chapter Eight

From the mess tent, Pearson watched the last of the exhausted crew unload from the trucks as they pulled into camp, their faces and clothing stained black from working in the smoke and sweat of the big burn up on Bison Ridge. It had taken three days of pick and shovel work to put the lightning strike fire out. The blaze had taken all four of the Wild Wind Motor Lodge guest cabins along with the twelve hundred acres of prime timber. Most of the men, too tired to eat, slowly walked past like soot-covered ghosts on their way to the showers. They were now earning every nickel of the thirty dollars a month paid by the government.

Pearson had only been the lead forest service team supervisor for a week prior to the fire, and it had been the first time he had seen this particular crew in action, a daunting proposition when lives were on the line. He was the man in charge of all hundred and forty men of Camp 45 of the Civilian Conservation Corp or CCC. He was the man responsible for putting men on the fire line.

The Corp, the brainchild of the current Roosevelt Administration, was a desperate attempt to stop the crushing blight of Depression era unemployment by putting hundreds of thousands of unemployed men onto massive public work projects funded totally by the government. Bridges, dams, highways, and forest protection all fell under the CCC mandate.

A week ago, his first impression of the new crew was one of quiet concern. The men seemed to lack the motivation to maintain even basic CCC guidelines of personal grooming and uniform standards, standards written and patterned after the military. In addition, the first inspection of the camp tent compound had been less than stellar; nothing had been lined up according to regulation. But after seeing this rough-around-the-edges group of civilians work sixteen hour days in blistering heat and smoke without one word of complaint, his impression had changed. This was a group that could match any Spike Fire Crew anywhere in the country. As far as he was concerned, the men in his charge could wear their beards and hair as long as they wanted if they kept fighting fires like they had this past week. It had been an amazing effort.

"Jesus, that was a kick in the nuts," announced Mike Shoen, stepping into the tent and heading for the coffee urn. Shoen was one of the fire service's five crew-leads at the camp. A ten-year veteran of the department, his massive physical stature, heavy black beard, and booming voice carried all the authority he needed to maintain control of the men under his command. Pearson watched the big man walk by trailing a heavy smell of wood smoke and sweat. He was 'one of those guys,' a nearly mythical hitter that on occasion crosses paths with the rest of the mere mortals, a hard case, another one of the crazy brave. He had seen the big man wade into a hair-burning ground fire with nothing more than a shovel and walk out after digging a fire-break that normally would have taken three men to dig.

"How's it look up there, Mike?" he asked. Shoen sat down heavily on the table bench, the fatigue pressed deep in the lines of his face. "Took us all afternoon to clear out all that beaver bait near the road. Thought we'd never get that pile of shit put out." He stuffed a biscuit in his mouth. "Got the skidder in just after lunch and stacked a cold deck just off the access road."

"Everybody okay? No injuries?"

Shoen shook his head and stuffed in another cold biscuit. "Naw, you can't hurt them high-ballers. Good bunch of fellas. Fun to watch 'em work. How's the kid?"

"Getting ready to go check on him now," replied Pearson pushing away from the table. "Talked to the doc earlier. Said he thinks he's gonna make it. Tough little bastard."

Shoen nodded. "Lucky that we found him when we did. We were just about to start setting a back burn in that ditch he was in."

Pearson set his empty coffee cup in the wash tray. "I'm gonna head on over to the dispensary now. I'll let you know what I find out."

Shoen nodded and stuffed in a third biscuit. "Okay."

Pearson turned before walking out of the tent. "Hey, Mike."

"Yeah."

"Get some sleep. You look like shit."

Shoen just smiled, stuffing in another biscuit as Pearson stepped out of the tent on his way to the dispensary.

****

Penny eased back on the bed after taking a long sip of the strong coffee. He still did not have much of an appetite, having just regained consciousness the night before. His feet were heavily bandaged and a thick pad was taped to his back just below his left shoulder blade. The tall skinny doc had told him that he was in a CCC camp just outside of Missoula. Past that, not much other information had been offered. He carefully adjusted the pillow behind his neck, trying to get the pressure off his back as a man he had not seen before walked in. To Penny, the man carried himself like someone in charge.

"Evening, young man," he announced stepping close to the bed. "How you feeling?"

"Okay, I guess. My feet hurt. How did I get here? Where am I?"

Pearson pulled up one of the small chairs. "Well, it's a pretty lucky story for you. My name's Pearson, Bob Pearson. And you are?" he asked extending his hand.

"Penny Reynolds."

"Interesting name you got there, Penny."

"It's short for Pendleton. Named after my granddad. How did I get here?"

Pearson smiled, "Well, like I said, you were lucky."

Penny grimaced while adjusting his back on the mattress. "Don't feel too lucky right now."

Pearson laughed. "I beg to differ, young man. You got struck by lightning. The bolt came through your feet and punched a nickel size hole out your back. Never seen anything like it. You should've been a gonner."

Penny thought for a moment trying to remember anything prior to yesterday. "How did I get here?"

Pearson sat back in his chair. "The bolt that hit you started one hell of a fire. One of my crews was sent out to take care of it. That's where they found you face down in a ditch. They picked you up and brought you here. Our doc was closer than the one in town. He's the one that fixed you up."

Penny raised up on one elbow. "I had a suitcase. Is it here?"

Pearson reached into his coat pocket and pulled out a singed brown paper bag. "Didn't find a suit case. Fire got it, I suspect, but you had this in the coat pocket. That coat was probably the one thing that saved your life. It burned but you didn't. This was in the pocket."

He handed the bag to Penny. "Little over seventy dollars by my count. Thought you might want it back. A sizeable sum."

Relieved, Penny took the bag. "So what now?" he asked. He wasn't about to bring up the pistol.

Pearson slapped his knees and stood up. "Well, let's take a few more days to get you back on your feet, and then we can decide what you need to do next. We can start contacting your kin in the meantime, let them know you're okay."

"Don't have any kin," he replied lying back down with a sigh. "My folks are both dead."

Pearson shook his head. "Sorry to hear it. You don't have anyone we can contact? Aunts, uncles, brothers, sisters, anyone?"

"No, sir. I am by myself. No one else."

Pearson thought for a moment. A young kid like this up here by himself raised a whole lot more questions than answers. "How old are you anyway?"

"Seventeen." It was a lie of course; he wouldn't be seventeen for four months.

"Hmm, seventeen, huh? You look about fifteen if I had to guess."

Penny lay back on the bed, trying to ease the building pain in his back. He didn't like where the conversation was headed. "Don't know what to tell ya'. Give me a day or so, and I'll move on."

Pearson smiled. The kid was a mess but was playing the hard case routine pretty well. For a moment he thought about asking him why he was carrying the pistol but checked the question for another time. The boy wasn't going anywhere soon as banged up as he was. No, he'd talk to him later and find out the real story behind the kid with the fresh Lichtenberg scar on his back. He had time.

"All right, Penny. Get some sleep. I'll talk to you tomorrow. Doc will be in to check on you later."

As he left, he sensed that the kid wanted to say something or even hear something. He was alone, afraid, and hurt, a tough combination for anyone. It was amazing he was even alive. He would give him some time to settle down.

He left the tent and stood on the porch platform lighting a cigarette as a cool gust of pine-scented air blew through the compound. Across the way he could see the glow of a hundred kerosene lamps inside the corp tents, casting a comforting orange glow through the canvas roofs. The men were settling down for the night. Many were already in an exhausted sleep from fighting the fire.

This was his favorite time of day in the camp, just after sunset. The sound of the cicadas in the trees and the cool mountain air brought a comfort to his heart that was almost spiritual. Montana had put the hook in him early. Big Sky Country they called it, a handle that didn't even come close to what it really looked like standing on the bluffs just outside of Missoula watching the sunrise over the Bitterroots. Watching those expansive purple, orange and then brilliant rays of golden light fill the horizon was like watching God open the front door to heaven. Anyone standing in that magical first light became a Believer, leaving him changed forever. Montana - for him, the name said it all. He would never leave.

Chapter Nine

Mitch Edwards stood in the open door of the descending DC-3 as the tree covered peaks of the north central Montana Mission mountains slowly rolled by underneath. This was the third run on the drop zone. Having already kicked out two test bundles to check the wind drift in the prior runs, in this pass - he would be the bundle. He removed his headset and grabbed the inside door rungs, easing himself out into the roaring slipstream for a pre-jump look, the cold hundred-mile-an-hour wind tearing at his clothes.

Pulling himself back inside, he raised his goggles and retrieved his headset. "Hey, Mike, give me about five degrees to the left. I wanna stay out of the trees if I can."

Mike Stovall, the young pilot who had just gotten on with the Forestry Service out of Missoula made the slight correction. "Roger that, Mitch. Gonna power down to just above stall - on your mark," he replied through his headset. Doing a quick calculation, he knew that he needed to constantly be aware of the ambient altitude density before he started reducing the prop rpms to 2550. Stall speed for the DC-3 was sixty-five to sixty-eight knots but at the AGL of the drop zone, which was right at four thousand feet, he would need to stay at around 2,300 rpms with thirty-six inches of manifold pressure to stay airborne. Bottom line, anyone going out the side cargo door was in for a hundred-and-ten mile-an-hour prop blast, a pretty heavy body blow for anyone. "Twenty seconds, Mitch," he announced over the radio. "Can't slow it down too much."

"Didn't think so," replied Mitch hooking up his static line to the heavy cable that ran close to the top of the aircraft ceiling. "Give me a green light, will ya? I'm hanging up the headset."

"You got it. Stand by. Winds out of the northeast three to five knots."

Mitch adjusted his goggles and stepped close to the door's edge, checking to be sure his static line was clear. Just before he heard the right-side prop change pitch, he felt an incredible nervous energy surge through his body when the small green "go" light suddenly blinked on. Instantly, he pushed himself out into the howling slipstream dropping the full twelve feet of static line.

The wind rush and noise was incredible as he swung violently forward and then backward, the deployment bag and suspension lines ripping out of the container. In seconds the opening shock from the thirty-foot conical main parachute slammed him into a mid-air stop, knocking the wind from his lungs and his goggles from his face.

"Jesus Christ," he grunted looking up to check the main. Out of the four jumps he had made this week, this had been the heaviest opening shock. He could not remember a time in his life when he had been slammed so hard.

Slowly catching his breath, he looked down past his boots at the dark green drop zone 1800 feet below. It had been a good exit spot, putting him out way left of the trees where he had landed two days ago. That landing in the old growth pines had put a deep six-inch long wound on the inside of his left thigh and a genuine fear of ever parachuting into trees again. He reached up and pulled down a double handful of suspension line riser allowing him to slowly turn the canopy 90 degrees. Now facing into the wind, he could see the bright orange wind sock on the far end of the DZ.

Studying the ground still a thousand feet below, he could see that he was slowly drifting backwards, a clear sign that the winds aloft were a lot stronger than the three to five knots Mike had announced. In fact, he was actually picking up speed, which meant several things - all bad. First, he knew he needed to be facing into the wind on landing. Secondly, it meant he would be doing a rear parachute landing fall or PLF, and third, a rear PLF at high speed always knocked the piss out of him.

At that moment, the seventy dollars a month he was getting paid by the government did not seem to be near enough money for what he was about to go through. He reached up and tightened the chinstrap on the leather football helmet knowing full well that no matter what he did to prepare for landing, it was still going to hurt.

Pearson stopped his pickup truck at the edge of the expansive meadow that the Seeley Lake Ranger Station had been using for a runway and drop zone. Over the last several months more and more aircraft had been landing at the remote site bringing in everything from building materials to communication equipment to fire suppression gear. In addition, it was now being stood up as the newly formed Smoke Jumper training and staging facility.

Smoke jumping, a highly controversial program, selected and trained crews to parachute onto the fire line, something that had never been done before. In Pearson's mind, anything that got the crews onto the fire quickly was a good thing, but he wasn't making the decisions. He was paid to implement the plan.

Sitting behind the wheel of his truck, he lit a cigarette and watched as his long time friend, Mitch Edwards, sailed by under canopy and then slammed into the short grass near the dirt strip runway twenty yards away. Even this far away it sounded like someone had dropped a hundred-pound sack of wheat onto wet concrete. Edwards had to be one tough son-of-a-bitch to do that for a living, he thought.

Amused, Pearson watched as Mitch slowly sat up, dazed and dirty from the hard landing. "That looked like fun. You need to suit up and do that again," he said, walking over smiling.

Mitch pulled his helmet off. "Jesus, didn't feel like fun," he said holding out his hand. "Here, help an old man up."

Person pulled him to his feet. "You do know that jumping out of perfectly good airplanes is never a good idea, right?" He handed him his already lit cigarette. "You really think this *smoke jumping* thing of yours is going to catch on?"

Mitch took a long drag before answering and then handed the smoke back. "Yeah, I do. Gotta cut the response time down on big burns," he replied unbuckling his harness. "What are you doing up here anyway besides throwing cold water on my program? Don't you have about a hundred city boys to wet nurse down in that *camp* of yours?"

Pearson laughed while helping him out of the rest of the gear. "Well, I came here to ask you a favor, Mitch, and it's a big one."

Edwards knelt down and started stuffing the jump harness into his gear bag. "And before you ask, I am not buying that goddamned old pickup of yours. That thing was beat to shit two years ago when you first tried to sell it to me."

Pearson laughed. "Naw, it's not the truck, Mitch. I've picked up a stray, and I'd like you to take him under your wing,"

Edwards eyed him suspiciously. "Why me? What's wrong with him?"

Pearson picked up the gear bag Mitch had just packed. "C'mon. I'll give you a ride back to that rat hole shack of yours. It's a pretty good story. Besides, I'm your boss so you have to listen to me."

In reality, Mitch had never really wanted a position of authority within the fire service at all. Throughout his life he had chased adventure, from working as a big game hunting guide in Zambia to cross country automobile racing for the Bugatti racing team, grueling car endurance races popular all over the world in the late twenties. On one of his many trips to Europe, he had gone to the Paris air show out of curiosity. On an overcast afternoon in 1935, on the last day of the event, he watched several members of the *Avignon-Pujaut Paratroopers* conduct a demonstration jump onto the expansive grass field near the main exposition hall. It was an event that would change his life.

The school for parachuting had been founded by the diminutive yet flamboyant Captain Geille, a legend and balls-to-the-wall ace with the French Air Force during the Twenties. From this organization in the early days of World War Two, the French military had trained and equipped two combat airborne units designated *Groupes d'Infanteire de l'Air*, a unit that suffered horrendous losses during the war.

Mitch had been immediately fascinated by the parachutists and vowed to learn everything he could about this new technology. By 1937, he had made over fifty jumps, having received a rudimentary course in Belgium. In the fall of thirty-eight, he migrated back to the States due to the building conflict throughout Europe. War was coming to the playground, and nobody wanted to be caught out in the open when it arrived, especially a free-spirited American who loved French women, fine wine and the unrestricted time to chase both.

Using his aviation contacts in the States, he had been hired to work with the newly formed *Forestry Aviation and Fire Watch Patrol*, currently being developed in the western part of the country, a predecessor to the United States Forestry Service. His timing for an occupational shift could not have been more perfect. Smoke Jumping had been his idea, and he now had funds and the governmental nod to develop it.

For oversight, Seeley Lake Ranger Station Montana fell under Pearson's area of operation and control, which meant all the assets, including the crazy guy with lots of government money who jumped out of airplanes, worked for him.

Mitch shook his head, thinking about what Pearson had just told him. "So this kid lost both parents, his father shot down on the front porch, and the mom died from the dust?" he asked, handing Pearson a beer from the small cooler.

"Yep, took a week and a half for the law in Kansas to get back to me about him," replied Pearson sitting down on the porch. "Evidently he was there when his old man got shot. A couple of days later, after the funeral, he grabs what little he's got, jumps a freight and ends up here. Oh and by the way, as if the kid's luck wasn't bad enough, he got struck by lightning last week, damn near killed him. That fire up on Bison Springs was caused by the strike that hit him."

Mitch took a long drink of his beer and then belched. "What am I suppose to do with him? He's just a kid."

"I don't know, maybe teach him how to refuel airplanes," replied Pearson.

"They do that in Missoula."

"Okay, show him the ropes on Smoke Jumping."

Mitch thought for a moment. "How old did you say he was?"

Pearson smiled. "Sixteen going on twenty-five. Listen, Mitch, he really doesn't have any place to go. Hell, use him to clean up the station, kind of like a permanent caretaker." He looked around, "God knows, it could use it."

Mitch shook his head. "What's he going to do when the snow hits? I'm heading down to California for the winter. What then? I can't take him down to Lockheed."

Pearson drained the last of his beer and tossed the empty into the bucket by the door. "Kid's gonna be seventeen in three months, which as you know, is old enough to join CCC."

"But he's a minor right now, right?" questioned Mitch.

Pearson looked up as a large flock of Canadian geese squawked by high overhead, a sound that always made him smile. "Yeah, he's a minor. I plan on giving him fire watch duty all winter, have him work with Paul Miller over in Sula. By spring he will be old enough for anything we have to offer. I could even put him on a crew if I have to.

Mitch thought for a moment. "You like this kid, huh?"

Pearson smiled, "Yeah, I do. He's a tough little bastard. But the boy needs a break. Hell, I got a whole camp full of guys I'm watching over already. I don't see much difference with bringing in one more. I think this is what I am supposed to do."

Mitch tossed his empty beer bottle in the bucket shaking his head. Though he would not admit it, this was one of the things he liked about Pearson. True compassion was a rare thing in these hard times. People were doing everything they could just to stay alive and sometimes even that wasn't enough. In Pearson's case, it was not an act; it was real.

"Okay, Bob, send the kid up. He can bunk in the small cabin over there. He'll have to share with the pilots during the week but they all head back to Missoula on the weekends."

Pearson nodded. "Thanks, Mitch. I'll go run the plan by him, see what he thinks. He's still laid up in the infirmary."

"Jesus, Bob, you haven't talked to him yet? Hell, what if he wants to run off and play baseball, chase girls, shit, I don't know, maybe join the circus or something?"

Pearson stood up and stepped off the porch laughing. "Not that kind of kid, my friend. I think he's gonna be pretty solid. You'll see that hard edge when you meet him."

Mitch leaned back in his chair still not sure what he was about to get himself into. "You think you can convince him to go with your plan?"

Pearson turned and smiled. "Hell, that's gonna be easy, pard. You were the one I was worried about."

Chapter Ten

It was just after six in the evening when Penny hobbled up onto the mess tent porch and walked inside, the large tent full to the walls with men talking and eating at several long tables and benches. The smell of cornbread, strong coffee, and red beans hung heavy in the air as he walked up and picked up a metal tray off the stack.

"Keep the line moving, gents," announced the man wearing a white apron, standing behind the long serving counter. "Let's go. Keep it moving."

Penny slid his tray under the glass partition letting another man drop a large spoonful of beans in the middle. Another server dropped a large block of corn bread in the beans and then handed the tray back. "Lets go. Keep it moving."

Easing through the crowd, he found an empty spot on a bench by the back door and took a seat. As he looked around at the crush of diners, he was surprised to see that most of the men seemed to be about the same age - thirty to forty-five years old, men close to his father's age. The sudden memory of his father sent a physical pain through his chest just above his heart. Tears welled up in his eyes as he fought the emotion, the last thing he wanted these men to see. He realized he was the youngest person in the tent, making him feel as if every eye was on him. Crying would do nothing to improve their perceptions.

"Hey, I'm glad to see you up and about."

Penny turned to the voice as Pearson slid in beside him with his tray.

"Mind if I sit here?"

"Suit yourself," replied Penny, taking in a mouthful of beans.

A low peel of distant thunder rumbled through the air. "Looks like it's getting ready to come down," announced Pearson sipping his coffee.

This was only the second time Penny had spoken to or even seen Pearson since he had arrived a full week ago.

"How's your feet?" Pearson asked.

"I'm okay; just sore that's all. Doc says I can wear my shoes again."

"That's good, real good. Hey listen. When you get done here, meet me back at the infirmary. Got a few things I want to talk to you about."

Penny fought the sudden feeling of panic beginning to rise in his stomach. Whenever someone wanted to *talk* to him it always meant something bad, something they wanted him to do that he wouldn't like. He was now regretting even telling Pearson his name or that he was from Kansas. For all he knew, the deputy who questioned him about the missing revolver was on his way to pick him up and take him back.

Pearson leaned over and smiled as if he had read his mind. "It's okay, Penny. You're safe here. I talked to your county commissioner back in Kansas. Told me all about what had happed to your folks."

Penny thought for a moment. "I ain't going back. There's nothing for me there."

Pearson nodded. "Yeah, I know. That's what we're going to talk about. I've got some ideas I think you might agree to."

Penny pushed the tray away. "I ain't going to no state home neither. Not gonna be locked up."

Pearson shook his head and laughed. "Jesus, Penny, nobody is getting locked up. Relax, will ya? I said you're safe here and I meant it."

A hard rain began to fall, filling the cool air with the smell of wet pine. On the horizon, brilliant purple blue flashes of far away lighting lit the night sky. A low thunder followed.

It would be well after midnight before the two had finished talking about the future. For Penny, it was if he had gone to church and received a gift from the Almighty Himself. He would have a job, a place to stay, and safety. A new chapter in his life was about to be written, one that cut away all the bad luck and fear, giving him a clean slate.

That night in the dark, as he lay in his bunk listening to the rain pound down, he let the images of his mother and father run through his mind. There had been good days before the dust came, summer nights lying in his bed listening to his parents, their murmurs and gentle laughter in the next room, comforting sounds of home that said all was right with the world and that all the promises of good things ahead would come true. Minutes later, as he dozed off to sleep, he could almost hear his parents in the next room.... almost.

***

Fifty-five-hundred miles to the east, Hans Minor, twenty-one-year-old Private Hans Minor of the *Leibstandarte SS Adolf Hitler unit (LSSAH)*, tightened the chin strap on his helmet as a deep rut in the road jolted the troop truck he was riding in hard enough to shoot a pain up his back. Several of the other SS riding with him in the dark swore and groaned from the pounding. If he didn't know better, he'd think the driver, Klaus Vetch, a wild-eyed punk from Dusseldorf was trying to hit every pothole he could just for the fun of it.

Vetch, what a terrible name, thought Hans holding onto his rifle as they hit another deep rut. "Fucking Vetch!" shouted one of the SS from the dark. Hans smiled as the soldier angrily flipped open the canvas partition between the cab and the back of the truck. He reached through and grabbed the driver roughly by the neck. "Slow down, you piece of shit."

Vetch slapped his hand away. "Fuck off," he shouted back. "I have to keep up with the rest of the convoy. You're lucky you're riding and not walking, pretty boy."

"Let it go," commanded a voice from the dark of the truck. Hans immediately recognized the deep voice of Sgt. Dietz, one of the new NCOs recently assigned to the unit. No one knew much about him other than he had once been regular Army and that he was from some shit-heel town in northern Germany called Geritz. He carried himself with a quiet, almost solemn demeanor that was unusual for SS NONCOMS.

In Hans' mind, most of the NCOs he had had dealings with back in Bad Tolz had been sadistic bastards, men who got real enjoyment watching their underlings suffer. None of them had been in the Hitler Youth Program like he had which immediately disqualified them from any leadership position in his mind. Most of his training instructors had been regular Army laterally transferred to the SS as instructors for the six-week training rotations, a bunch of half-wit thugs as far as he was concerned, men he would not piss on if they were on fire.

As he sat in the back of the darkened truck, he had to remind himself that this was not an exercise, not some mindless drill concocted by the training cadre. This was the real thing, and no matter how much rain, mud, or distance he had to endure, he was about to use the skills he had learned. Within two hours, he would be killing people- Poles to be exact, individuals he considered to be on the same sub-level as Jews.

Their objective was to secure the railway station in the city of Morka. His unit was part of a three-pronged attack that would sweep the city eastward, crush all resistance, and then hold the town until Army regular units from the Tenth Panzer Division rolled in.

As if the spine-jolting ride in the dark could not get more miserable, one of the other SS Sergeants sitting next to him farted loudly, instantly filling the air with a putrid smell that brought groans and curses from the tightly packed men.

"I swear to God!" shouted someone seriously in the dark. "The next son-of-a-bitch that does that.... I will shoot him."

For a moment the truck was silent, but as if on queue, someone else let out an even louder more noxious fart that brought howls of laughter.

"Fucking animals!" shouted the same voice which only brought more laughter and groans.

For Hans, it was as if all the tension and fear he had been feeling the past several days suddenly spilled out in nearly uncontrolled hysterical laughter. He felt an incredible emotional release as tears rolled down his cheeks. For the first time since he had climbed into the truck that pre-dawn morning, he was grateful for the dark. The SS did not cry..... never.

Chapter Eleven

It had been a full two and a half weeks since Pearson had driven him up to the Sealy Lake Station. The days had been getting colder, and Penny had spent most of his time cutting and stacking a nearly endless supply of wood for the station's three wood stoves. He had also been tasked with general cleanup of both his and the main cabin. Edwards had told him what needed to be taken care of and then let him pretty much plan his day to get it done.

His foot had healed along with the other injuries from the lightning strike, allowing him to put in good steady twelve-hour workdays swinging a Collins axe, work that was turning soft palm callouses into leather-like pads. He could feel himself getting stronger by the day.

The best part of his job was being able to watch the planes come in, loading up the airdrop bundles and then retrieving the same bundles in and around the airfield after all the practice drops. He could never get tired of watching the big DC-3 drop in over the eastern range, slow to almost stall speed, and then drop all the parachuted rigged boxes. For a teenager from Kansas who had never seen an airplane in real life, the airdrops were a wonder to watch.

It was just before sunset when Edwards walked into the main cabin of the station with three other pilots. Penny had been helping the cook as he had since his arrival, shuttling plates and food back and forth from the kitchen. Another thing he really liked about working at Sealy - the food was great and there was plenty of it. The cook, a young CCC line cook by the name of Ross Pentair, a tall skinny red-haired guy, was not much older than Penny and had been hired on for the summer season.

As the men sat down, Penny pulled up his chair and ate, listening to Edwards and the pilots talk about the day's activities. He could listen to the men talk about wind currents, aircraft aerodynamics, and parachute rigging for hours. He was getting a glimpse of a whole new fascinating world, and he could not get enough of it. He admired the pilots and the ease at which they talked about the complexities of flying the big Douglas. It was a sureness of purpose and ability that struck a deep cord with him.

Later that night, as the men drank their coffee, the conversation shifted from flying to current political events. "Did you read the paper yesterday?" questioned one of the pilots easing back in his chair. "Germany invaded Poland."

Edwards, particularly animated by the discussion, nodded while lighting a cigarette. "Yeah, I saw it. Looks like all of Europe is about to get involved. The statement cast a pall over the conversation, the men growing quiet, each weighing the enormity of coming events. War was raging in Europe and each man sitting at the table knew in his gut that it was just a matter of time before it involved them all. The sense of inevitability hung heavy in the air. Outside, a light snow began to fall sending a natural hush through the trees.

Winter had arrived and would stay until middle March. The rivers would freeze and the pack ice on the high ridges of the Saw Tooth Mountains, where only the wind and the big horn sheep moved, would turn an off-shade of blue from the cold. The cycle of life this high cared nothing for the affairs of men. Wars, heartache, and strife blew through the trees, disappearing in the cold mist rising off the Salmon River like it had never happened.

***

Later that night, as Penny rolled into his blankets, he thought about the events that had brought him to the mountains and how his situation had improved. He was working - making a wage. He had a roof over his head and a bed to sleep in. He was getting fed and the men he was working for were men he respected, even admired. After listening to Edwards and the pilots talk tonight, he had become more certain than ever of what he wanted to do. In the morning he would ask Edwards if he could become a Smoke Jumper - go through the newly formed program, learn how to fight fires and jump out of planes. In his mind it was a perfect fit, and he knew his father would have approved.

Outside, the wind picked up, blowing a low whistling sound through the windowsill, the dropping temperature making the cabin snap and creak. As he lay listening to the wind, he tried to remember what his mother's face looked like. He could see the faded blue dress she always wore with the tiny yellow flowers around the neck. He could see her shoes, black three-hole lace-ups with the heels run down, the same shoes all the older women wore in his town. It was like a uniform now that he thought about it.

He remembered the small maroon-colored velvet hat she wore to church. She had kept it wrapped in tissue paper in a box on her closet shelf. It was probably still there. He let that memory go. Some things were just too sad to think about on a cold stormy night. His mother would understand, he thought, slowly nodding off to sleep.

****

They had been shooting people and getting shot at for three days now and still the Panzer units had not shown up. The tank platoons that were supposed to be the rear vanguard for the entire operation were still seven miles out of town. What little radio traffic that had been picked up said the tanks had encountered heavier than expected resistance and that they were *actively engaged*. In plain language, the Tenth Panzer Division that was supposed to be rolling in with Hans' SS unit was wrapped up in a bloody fight with half a regiment of the Polish 2nd Core, a hard-edged force that had been unwilling to give up an inch of Polish soil.

The fighting had been horrific - close quarter, pistol range contact where you saw your rounds hit - close enough to see the blood fly. Casualties on both sides were tremendous and growing by the hour.

All of this, of course, was unknown to Hans and the rest of his company who had blown through the streets of Morka, killing anything that had even remotely posed a threat, and then securing the railway station with ease. For the last two and a half days, Hans' platoon of thirty-two had been fighting a running gun battle with an unknown number of Polish regulars. They had beaten them back twice only to have them regroup and counter attack with sledgehammer ferocity.

Polish mortars and small, highly mobile artillery had been blasting the railway station to bits all morning, a barrage that had killed one of Hans' close friends, Christen Kline, a tall rangy kid with almost silver-blond hair and eyebrows so light it looked like he did not have any. He had been with him since Bad Tolz. His father, a Munich print shop owner who drank too much, had beaten Christian's mother to death a week before he had shipped out on this operation.

The older Kline had been arrested by the Gestapo that night, taken to the nearest police station on the west end of Munich, and drowned in a toilet commode with the help of two SS officers who had shown up unannounced. The SS took care of their own. The body had been dropped in the river before dawn, no questions asked.

Just after four in the afternoon on the second day of fighting, Hans had seen Christian running across a gap between several smoking boxcars and the pile of rubble that had once been the Station Master's office when a shell hit nearly on top of him. For a split second his lanky frame had been visible in the bright orange light of detonation, arms out stretched, his feet three feet off the ground, and then he was gone, vaporized by the blast.

Christian had been a good friend, and in his rage, Hans had shot the three Polish prisoners as they sat crying in the mud, dazed and beaten from the day's fighting. He had tied their hands behind their backs with telephone wire when they were first captured, making sure it was tight enough to turn their hands blue. He had made them sit back to back in the mud near the edge of the road, out in the open, actually wanting to see if shrapnel from the mortar barrage would hit them. But after watching Christian get blown to bits, the game had changed. From his position behind the broken stone and rubble thirty yards away, he had taken careful aim and shot each one of them in the head. *Like shooting ripe pumpkins on a post*, he had thought. Ironically enough, just after he had killed the third man, a Polish shell had landed nearly on top of the bodies, scattering their remains like shredded rags all over the street.

"Minor!" Sergeant Dietz had announced from behind his own rock and debris barricade thirty feet away. "Stop shooting the goddamned prisoners." It had sounded not so much like a command but an exhausted request from a man who had slept maybe two hours in three days. "Can't spare the ammunition."

Hans rested the front of his helmet on the sand bag, the smell of urine-soaked burlap filling his nostrils. He had been in and out of this fighting position since they had taken the station days ago. Due to the heavy shelling, it had been his only safe place to piss. In the street, acrid smoke from the recent shelling drifted overhead, the bodies of the prisoners making an odd pop and snapping sound as their fat smoldered and burned.

"You have any water?" asked Hans, his head still resting on the sand bag.

"What?" replied Dietz.

"I said, do you have any water? I'm dry."

Dietz tossed a half full canteen over to Hans' position. "Don't take it all. No telling when we will get resupplied."

Hans took several deep swallows and then tossed it back. "How long can we hold out?" he asked slumping down into his hole.

Dietz chuckled. "Til we are all dead. Why? Do you have some place you need to be?"

Hans laughed as another heavy mortar round crashed into the roof of the Sweetshop across the street. The thunderous blast seemed to suck all the oxygen out of the air. He quickly got to his knees, peering out of the shooting port he had made of sand bags and rock as the smoke drifted across his position. Forty yards away, five Polish troops suddenly made a mad sprint across the street and into what was left of a small bakery. He was able to get off one shot at the group that missed before they disappeared behind the rubble.

He quickly racked the bolt on his rifle, wincing in pain from the deep cut on his palm. Yesterday on a run from the station back to his position, he had tripped in some wire and fallen on a shard of glass. The shit was everywhere. The wound had been bothering him ever since.

These were the things in war nobody talked about during training, the little things that wore you down in small increments, like not being able to take a proper shit in a comfortable place. When you finally did let it go, it was like it would never stop. They didn't talk about the small wounds you got from diving on the ground or running into things as you scrambled over rubble trying to stay alive, the small painful injuries that only began to hurt hours after you got them. There were no close-combat patches or medals for those, only tiny scars that brought it all back in a rush years later in life.

He found it amazing how quickly you were filthy, your uniform caked with mud, sweat, and sometimes your own blood. He was equally amazed at how the discomfort all went away the second the shooting started, that strange high-pitched noise heard just above the sound of your own breathing. For Hans, the exhilaration of combat was magical, almost a spiritual experience. Nothing he had seen or done in the last three days had shaken his belief that the SS was where he needed to be.

This was what he had been looking for. This is what he had wanted. All the marching in the Hitler Youth, walking on blisters till they bled, all the war games with wooden rifles and the midnight fistfights, all of it had put a sharp, definable edge on his soul. Even though this was the first time he had seen combat, the blood and the carnage seemed oddly familiar; his conditioning to killing had been successful.

As he knelt in his own piss waiting for another shot at the men behind the rubble fifty yards away, he felt neither fear nor remorse. As he wiped the sweat out of his eyes, he felt only a growing fatigue that had settled between his shoulder blades. At ground level, there was no indication that the bloody stalemate between the two forces now fighting over the town would ever end, but if one stood in the shattered remains of the Orthodox church's bell tower that over looked the city's main square, you would see the first two Tiger tanks from the German Tenth Division rumbling up the street. The Panzers had arrived.

Now the real slaughter would begin.

Chapter Twelve

It had been two days since Penny had approached Edwards with the idea that he wanted to be a Smoke Jumper and learn everything he could about the program. Edwards had been non-committal saying only that he would have to think about it and would let him know. After three days, not having any further discussion about his idea, Penny started to let the thought go and concentrated on his daily chores, wood splitting and general clean up around the station. Snow was coming daily now and most of the flights from Missoula were either delayed or cancelled outright, and he missed seeing the big Douglas drop in over the ridge and roar to a stop on the now snow covered strip. It was something he had looked forward to everyday.

It was late Friday afternoon and Penny was stacking his last cord of wood by the cabin when he heard the familiar sound of the DC-3 coming in from the east. The day had been clear, the sky a deep blue, glorious for mid October.

Edwards stepped out onto the porch, zipping up his heavy coat and pulling on his gloves. "Hey, Penny!" he called.

Penny stepped out from around the corner of the building. "Yeah?"

"I've been thinking about what you said about the Smoke Jumper idea."

Penny wiped his runny nose on his sleeve, steeling himself for bad news. "Okay."

"Were you serious? I mean, you're pretty young to be making such a big decision."

Penny thought for a moment. "How old were you when you started chasing something you really wanted?"

Edwards chuckled. "About your age. You do know you can get killed doing this job?"

Penny nodded. "So?"

"So, I just want you to know that jumping out of airplanes and fighting fires is a very dangerous occupation."

Penny smiled. "Not as dangerous as riding freights."

Edwards pulled a cigarette out of his coat's inside pocket and lit it, the smoke hanging in the still air. "You get killed, Penny, it's gonna be on me, you know. I'm responsible."

Penny could hardly believe what he was hearing. "So what are you saying?"

Just then, the silver DC-3 dropped onto the far end of the strip, the engine's noise and pitch feathering back. Edwards took a long drag, watching the bird roll up through the three-inch deep snow. "Well. I think it's time you took a ride. Maybe that will scare some sense into ya. Go put that axe away and get your heavy coat. Gonna be cold on top."

It had been just over three months since he had grabbed his suitcase and jumped out of Pastor Kline's bedroom window that hot dusty day in Kansas. Now, he could barely contain his excitement as he followed Edwards to the idling DC-3, the massive props spinning nearly invisible in the cold air.

A man dressed in heavy leather and fleece overhauls appeared in the open cargo door above them and lowered a small steel ladder. "Climb on up!" shouted Edwards above the engine noise. "Let's go."

The crewman grabbed Penny's arm and helped him into the plane and then motioned for him to take a seat on the web bench that ran along the far side of the fuselage. Inside, the smell of aviation exhaust was nearly overpowering. Edwards quickly climbed up the steps and patted the crewman on the shoulder as he stepped inside. "You okay?" he shouted to Penny, giving him thumbs up.

Penny smiled and nodded, returning the gesture. Must be a pilot thing, he thought watching the men pull up the ladder and close the cargo door. Edwards sat down next to Penny and showed him how to buckle his seat belt as the plane's engines throttled back up.

Minutes later the plane did a slow turn and then began a full throttle roar back down the strip. Penny watched out the window as the trees surrounding the runway flashed by. It was exhilarating and terrifying at the same time. Just when he thought the plane would shake apart, it lifted off the frozen ground and cleared the treetops at the far end of the field. Lord, if his folks could see him now, he thought as he watched the ground grow farther away. He was flying, something he never dreamed could happen.

"What do you think?" shouted Edwards above the engine noise.

Penny just shook his head and smiled, not able to find the words for how he felt. Edwards patted his leg and stood up. "If you feel like it, you can take the belt off and head up to the front with me!" he shouted hanging on to a steel cable overhead that ran the length of the fuselage. "Show you who is flying this thing."

For over an hour, Edwards showed Penny every inch of the inside of the DC-3 as they flew through the clear cold Montana sky, the bright sunlight coming through the portal windows on alternate sides as they changed direction. For Penny, the world had now opened doors to a place he never knew existed. To feel the plane drop and rise under his feet and to see the landscape below was practically a spiritual experience. His decision to be part of this world was now a certainty. This is where he belonged.

****

By eight o'clock in the morning of the seventh day of the invasion, most, if not all, Polish resistance had been crushed. The town of Morka now lay in ruin. Hundreds of dead lay scattered in the streets throughout the city. The fighting had been horrendous - visceral, up close, house-to-house warfare where no quarter had been given on either side. Prisoners had been shot along with the wounded, only stoking the blood-in-the-eye hatred.

This had been the first time the SS had been used as the "tip of the spear" forces in direct action, a decision that had resulted in tremendous casualties among the SS units. Later, there would be accusations that the commands had been ill-equipped and poorly led, leading to the abysmal casualty reports, information and after action statements from the field that infuriated Himmler, the man in charge of the SS and its main architect. Of course none of the finger pointing and political maneuvering above Hans' pay grade was any of his concern. In his mind and that of the survivors of his unit, they had done their job and were proud of the results. They had killed the enemy wholesale and anyone else, for that matter, that had stood in the way of their objective. There had been no hesitation, no moral second-guessing on their part. As loyal subjects of the Fuhrer, they had done their duty. Poland was now under the control of the Third Reich, a fact no one could argue with no matter what the body count.

In Hans' mind, if Polish civilians had been killed during the fight, it had been their bad luck to be in the line of fire. More importantly, it was their misfortune to have been born Poles in the first place. Gypsies, Poles, Jews, and Communists all fell under the sub-human category and in his way of thinking. It was no loss to the human race if they were all exterminated as quickly and as bloody as possible.

***

Hans stood under the hot shower rinsing away days of blood and filth from the operation. His unit had been relieved and was now back in Germany for resupply. This was the first shower he had had in over a week. According to Sergeant Dietz, a whole new group of NCO cadre and recent SS graduates would be augmenting his unit in the coming days. In Hans' mind it was just more fresh meat to feed into the grinder, an opinion that most of the returnees from the Polish operation shared. They had seen first-hand that this was not a campaign of Aryan ideals and moral superiority but a collective nervous breakdown with heavy firepower and enough blood lust to carry it out.

All the Nazi propaganda concerning the nobility of action in Poland and the higher calling of the cause vanished as fast as machine gun rounds zipped through the bodies of unarmed civilians in their front yards. Anybody who walked out of that burning, decimated city carried no illusions as to what was really going on. Hell had been unleashed and everyone in the world was going to get a taste.

****

For Penny, the flight in the DC-3 might as well have been a journey to another dimension, another reality. He was changed by the experience, pulled into a world of glowing possibilities.

Edwards had been impressed by how interested Penny had been in every facet of the aircraft and the down-to-the-bone excitement the kid exhibited in just being there. But now he was also going to have to tell him that there would be a change in plans in his smoke jumping, something he had been working up to ever since Pearson had let him know what the State of Montana had to say about an unaccompanied minor working at the Forestry Department. Edwards reread the notification letter again while sitting at the dining room table just to be sure he had his facts straight before Penny came back in from the kitchen.

It had been two days since the flight, and the weather had closed in, grounding all flights from Missoula. The only people left at the station now were the cook, Penny, and himself. Sadly, it would be one of the last meals they would all have together for some time. The cook walked into the dining room carrying a platter of elk steak and potatoes and took his seat. Penny followed him from the kitchen with the coffee pot and took his usual chair.

Penny could tell something was on Edwards' mind and was quietly praying it did not involve him, though in his gut he knew that it did.

"Hey, Penny," he said handing him the letter. "I've got something here you need to read. This has been bothering me for several days now. I figured we would take care of it tonight. Now, once you read it, we're going to talk about it and get some stuff figured out. No use ducking it."

Penny took the letter as if it were on fire, feeling as if all the oxygen had suddenly been sucked out of the room. Edwards leaned back in his chair with a sigh, his face expressing a mixture of concern and sadness. He nodded for Penny to read the letter.

September 17, 1939

Dear Mr. Pearson:

This letter is in response to your inquiry and our subsequent determination concerning the care and welfare of one Pendleton Charles Reynolds, a sixteen-year-old juvenile currently employed at the Sealy Lake Ranger Station. Through the information you have provided and our investigation, we have learned that Pendleton has no living parent or relative that could be responsible for his care.

He has a distant aunt in Des Moines, Iowa, but this person is unwilling or unable to take him in at this time. Because of the Fair Labor Legislation signed into law last year concerning specific work requirements for underage individuals, the States Attorney's Office has directed that Pendelton be mandated to the State of Montana Home for Boys in Missoula where he will finish his high school education and be under the proper care and guidance of child development professionals.

We would kindly request that you deliver the young man to the Admissions Office on the 25th of this month for his immediate enrollment in the fall quarter. Sister Margret Wilson, the School Administer and Head Master of the home will be awaiting your arrival.

Sincerely,

Harrison Hargrove,

State of Montana State Attorney's Office

Missoula, Montana.

Chapter Thirteen

Hans loaded a fresh magazine into the P40 machinegun still not sure if he was comfortable with the effectiveness of the weapon. Firing a nine-millimeter round and at a fairly fast rate of fire, the weapon should be decent in close quarter fighting but most, if not all, of his shots in Poland had been a good hundred to a hundred and fifty yards off. The last thing he wanted was to be shot at and not be able to shoot back due to range limits.

Sergeant Dietz walked up behind Hans on the firing line where most of the company had been re-zeroing their weapons all afternoon. "What do you think?" he asked sitting down on a pile of sand bags.

Hans folded the weapon's wire stock up and then fired the entire clip from the hip, churning up black sod divots twenty yards down range. He laid the weapon on a small table, shaking his head. "I don't know. It's fun to shoot but the lack of range bothers me. I think I like my rifle better."

Dietz lit a cigarette while leaning back on the sand bags. "Well, the platoon has been issued ten of them so somebody has to carry one."

Hans picked the weapon up. "So, is that an order? I have to carry this thing?"

Dietz blew a lung full of smoke in the air and chuckled. "Yes, I guess it is. You'll need to carry your rifle as well."

"Christ," replied Hans dropping the weapon back on the table.

"Hey, you're my best killer," announced Dietz smiling. "I figured you would want all the tools you could get for your work."

"What does that mean?" Hans asked, unbuttoning the top of his tunic. He wasn't sure if Dietz was mocking him or giving him some kind of left-handed compliment.

"I think you enjoyed Morka. I think you like pulling the trigger."

Hans held the Sergeant's gaze trying to see where this was going. "I like doing my duty, Sergeant. Carrying out orders is the most important thing to me."

Dietz smiled. "Oh, I think your actions in Morka went way beyond following orders. I saw you kill that old man, his two grand-daughters, along with the three prisoners. Very impressive shooting, I might add."

"You have something to say, Sergeant, I suggest you say it," announced Hans, feeling the heat rise in his face.

Dietz thought for a moment and then slowly stood up straightening his tunic. "What I am saying, Corporal, is that I admire your dedication and nerve. I did not come here to accuse you of anything, on the contrary. I hope the rest of the unit follows your example of dedication and ruthlessness when facing the enemy."

Hans still wasn't sure what Dietz was trying to say. As if the Sergeant had read his mind, he leaned close. "All I ask is that you be a little more *discreet* in your zeal. You can kill any Jew, Pole, Communist, or anyone else for that matter.

All I ask is that you do it without bringing attention to yourself or the unit. All right?"

Hans smiled. "Discreet?"

Dietz patted him on the shoulder as he turned to walk away. "We are God's avengers now, my young friend. We have much to do in His glorious service!" he shouted with a smile while walking backwards. "Take to heart what I said, Corporal." He turned and headed off into the woods behind the range, whistling a strange off-key tune that Hans had never heard before.

Excellent, he thought picking up the machinegun and loading in a fresh mag. Dietz had seen him commit murder and had said nothing about it other than to be more discreet in the future. He was surprised that there had been a clear witness to the shooting of the old man and the two little girls, moving targets that had been running hand in hand down one of the narrow alleys near the center of town. In all the chaos during the assault on the city, he was surprised that anyone had seen the fifty-yard shot.

He unfolded the stock on the P40 and this time took careful aim at the paper target. He smiled as he pulled the trigger realizing that Dietz wasn't quiet because of deep introspection and thought; he was quiet in demeanor because his was thoroughly insane, a condition that suited Hans perfectly. A kindred spirit is always nice to find.

****

It had been two weeks since the long drive down from Sealy Lake to the Montana Home for Boys in Missoula. Edwards had maintained an awkward silence most of the way, still not sure in his own mind that this was the right thing to do. He, himself had been getting ready to head to California and would be shutting down the station until spring. There simply hadn't been any other place for the kid to go.

As they had hit the Missoula city limit sign, Edwards had assured Penny that he would be able to come back up to the station in April. At seventeen and a half, he would be considered an adult in Montana at that point and could be part of the Smoke Jumping program if he still wanted it. Penny had told him that he would take him at his word and would be there the first day the station opened up. They had shaken hands and Edwards had driven away feeling as if he was leaving the scene of a crime.

***

The nuns who ran the home carried a pervasive air of stern compassion, one that promoted a sense of security and expectation of conduct at the same time. You knew from the moment you stepped in the door, what was expected as far as attitude and what was not.

Penny shared a third floor dormitory with sixteen other boys, a tough hard-edged group. He got along but did not go out of his way to associate with any of them unless he had to. Most, if not all of them had been in the State system most of their lives, institutionalized practically from birth. He learned that some had been abandoned; others had been beaten and abused, while others simply had no other place to go. They smoked stolen cigarettes when the nuns were out of sight, picked on the young ones who lived on the first and second floor, and in Penny's mind, lived lives of silly desperation. Though most of the boys were close to his age, they all seemed so much younger.

At the end of his first week, he had been challenged by the dorm's supposed shot-caller, Travis Dekes, a thickly built, red headed kid from Butte raised by the State of Montana having been the only survivor of a raging house fire that killed both his parents and two siblings. The confrontation had begun just before lights-out as Penny walked back from the large shower room. Dekes had been sitting on Penny's bunk in his underwear, picking through his suitcase.

The tension had been building for several days and when Penny saw Dekes pick up his mother's Bible and toss it on the floor, it had all come to a head. Dekes had barely gotten to his feet before Penny slammed into him with all the force he could muster, the impact sending them both flying through the air and landing with a thud on the hardwood floor on the other side of the bed.

Dekes, stunned by the impact, had struggled to his feet only to be kicked in the face, slamming him onto his back. Penny had then straddled the half conscious Dekes, raining down blow after blow as all the pent up fear, rage, and pain of the last three months exploded. Alarmed by the ferocity of the fight, the other boys had pulled Penny off, confident that Dekes would be beaten to death.

Later that night, after the blood on the floor had been cleaned, Penny lay in his bunk listening to the other boys quietly attending Dekes in the shower room down the hall. They had cleaned him up, dropped him in the bed and nothing else had been said about the matter. To Penny, the other boys had seemed strangely glad Dekes had gotten a beating; evidently scores had been settled the rest of them had been unwilling to address.

The next morning Dekes had looked like he had been run over by a truck. Both eyes had been nearly swollen shut and a deep split in his bottom lip would later need five stiches. It had been a sight that sent the Nuns into a shrieking panic, all demanding to know what had happened and who was responsible for such a terrible beating. To Penny's great surprise, no one said a word about the fight. Even more surprising, Dekes himself had said he fell in the shower. There were no snitches on the third floor, a tough code to live by but one that ruled the Montana State Home for Boys.

It was October when winter blew down from the Saw Tooths, dropping three feet of snow in below zero temperatures, a solid reminder that winter in western Montana is a force to be reckoned with. The winter of thirty-nine would be remembered as one of the worst on record. For Penny, he could care less how much it snowed or how cold it got; he knew what he was going to do in six months. Passing the time with a warm bed to sleep in with plenty of food to eat and a roof over his head was just fine with him. He was headed to the sky and nothing else really mattered. Let it snow.

Chapter Fourteen

Hans used his foot to slowly ease the red clay tile off the roof as he sat smoking a cigarette. Four floors below on the expansive grass-covered parade field, the new SS recruits were being put through a long set of mindless calisthenics of push-ups, sit ups, and jumping jacks, not so much for physical fitness but because the training cadre were half-drunk, bored and just wanted to see how many of the fresh young faces they could make vomit. Hans' unit, currently assigned to refit and resupply, was pretty much exempted from physical training other than weapons qualification. Now considered veterans, they were treated differently by the training cadre; a quiet air of respect connecting the training base staff and his unit.

As he nudged another tile off the roof, a low rumble of thunder rolled across the overcast sky. This was to be their last week on stand-down orders. A new operation was in the works with ammunition and equipment trucks arriving at the base every day in preparation for what was to come.

"Going to rain. I'm going inside," announced Mueller, one of the older privates transferred from Army to the SS just weeks before the Polish operation. "Dietz is probably going mad looking for us." He handed Hans the small flask of peach brandy and stood up, flicking his cigarette over the side. Since their mutual friend, Christian, had been blown to bits at the railway station, he and Hans had spent nearly every afternoon together on the roof of the administration building dodging Dietz, work details, and drinking peach brandy.

Mueller, from Bad Tolz, had grown up almost within sight of the building they now stood on. His father was a loyal party member who ran a small bread and meat market in town. His older brother was in the regular army out of Munich and was still somewhere in Poland.

Hans took a quick drink and handed the flask back. "I'm having bad dreams," he said wincing from the strong liquor that burned a ragged path down his throat.

Mueller took another drink and stuck the flask back in his coat pocket. "What kind of dreams?" knowing what Hans was getting at but not about to let him know that he had also been bothered by nightmares lately. He had cut back on the Pervitin methamphetamine that Dietz had been giving him every week, or Tank Chocolate pills as everyone called them. He had hoped that taking less would help stop the bad dreams but so far no luck. The NCOs handed them out like candy and when you were on it, you could stay awake and fight for days. Everyone in the SS and most of the regular army were taking the stuff. There was nothing like being high and pain free while killing people.

Hans shook his head watching the fifty recruits running around the large field in an exhausted formation down below. "Nightmares...burning bodies, people chasing me, and then my god-damn teeth falling out," he replied.

Mueller laughed. "That's an odd combination. Maybe you have a guilty conscience. Or worse, maybe you're jerking off too much."

Hans smiled and then thought for a moment, watching the dark blue storm clouds roll in from the east. "Yeah, maybe."

He stood up as several large drops of rain hit the dusty rooftop. "How are your dreams?" he asked, following Mueller to the open window, their rooftop access. He was trying hard to not sound too serious, though he was troubled by the nightly encounters, their intensity growing.

"I sleep like a puppy and when I dream," he pulled the curtains back laughing and ducked inside, "I dream of your sister. The things we do my friend....you would be shocked."

"She is out of your league," replied Hans following him in through the window as the rain started to fall in earnest. Mueller had never met his sister but had fallen in lust with her after seeing her picture. The way other boys and men had reacted to his sister's beauty had never bothered him growing up. Two years older, she was attractive, an attribute she had used to get what she wanted for years. Now with a much older man who bought her expensive chocolates and gifts, he knew she would continue to see him until he was out of money or when a better offer showed up.

In Hans' mind, you only got in life what you went out and took. He had watched how the years of doing the right thing had hammered his father down to a thin edge and then left him with nothing. For Hans, growing up on the gritty streets of lower south side Berlin with little more than his wits and the balls to fight for what he wanted had marked him early. The currency of his youth had been blood, mostly that of others. By sixteen he already become a headhunter in his neighborhood. By seventeen he had been a Hitler Youth team leader. The SS had just been a logical progression.

As they walked down the wide stone stairs of the building, their hobnail boots echoing through the hall, the training cadre could still be heard outside shouting commands to the exhausted recruits running in the rain. For a moment he thought about asking Mueller to give him a serious answer about how he had been feeling since their return from Poland. He wanted to know if anyone else was having night sweats or the odd fleeting images of people they had seen die walking around the compound. But then again, maybe he had already said too much.

He was fairly sure that Mueller wouldn't say anything about their conversation. It would not be good if the senior officers thought for a moment that one of their own was mentally impaired, though in Hans' mind, most, if not all of his superiors were borderline psychopaths, Dietz being at the top of the list. As they trotted through the rain across the courtyard on their way to barracks, Hans knew that whatever he was feeling about the Polish operation would have to stay buried. He would have to keep his own counsel, knowing that the less he talked about his feelings with other men, the safer he would be. If Mueller did start running his mouth, he would take care of the problem in the upcoming operation. Not every bullet is accounted for in the heat of battle making fixing a potential problem easy. It was a comforting thought that made him smile.

***

The holidays were the worst times at the Home for Penny but not because of anything the staff did or didn't do. They had tried hard to cheer everyone up but the festivities had only reminded him of all the good years he had had with his parents back in Kansas. When he sat in the big Catholic Church listening to sounds of Christmas Mass surrounded by the boys, staff, and all the trappings of joy and peace, he had never been more miserable. Even the new shoes that were a half size too big and the suit he had been given only served to remind him of his loss.

For the Nuns, seeing Penny cry affirmed a bedrock heartfelt belief that the beauty of the service with all its somber holy trappings had somehow touched the quiet young man, that his tears were that of contrition. If they had bothered to ask, they would have seen a young man who was broken and feeling more alone than anyone his age ever deserved to feel. Everyone he had ever loved was gone, his family now replaced by strangers paid by the State to care.

Penny had never been more relieved to have Christmas over. New Years came and went and in his mind - good riddance. 1940 was going to be his year.

Then the first signs of spring hit the west with a vengeance as it always had. The Bitterroot and the Salmon River broke up into a million tiny ice flows, tumbling and churning their way to Idaho. Most of the snowmelt in and around the city turned the roads into ankle high goo, something that had to be experienced to be appreciated. By May the trees began to blossom, grass began to turn green, and for the first time in months, people began to dig out of the emotional rut of the dark prolonged winter. Springtime in Montana was truly glorious.

Penny had told the nuns that he really did not want to be involved in the upcoming graduation ceremony. He had enough credits for his diploma and now he was ready to go. Besides, Edwards had left a message that he would be picking him up on the fifth of May and graduation was on the sixth.

Whenever Penny was asked about what he was going to do with his life after school, he always answered the question the same: "Going to jump out of planes and fight forest fires." The response to his answer was always akin to a blank look of incomprehension followed by a headshake and then a question like "Why would *anybody* jump out of an airplane?" Rarely would he explain himself further knowing that the person he was talking to couldn't begin to understand.

All that was important to Penny now was that Edwards showed up on the fifth. Past that, nothing else mattered. He could not allow himself to consider not getting back into the mountains; some things were just too terrible to think about.

On the evening of the fourth, Sister Miller, Head Master of the Home, called him into her office as he was walking down the hall just after supper. "Mister Reynolds, can I have a word please?" she asked softly.

"Yes, Ma'am." He stepped into the dark wood paneled office that smelled vaguely of mothballs and old books. In the months he had been at the Home, this was only the second time he had been in the office or even spoken to Sister Miller for that matter. She was not one of his teachers and he had not been a discipline problem, other then knocking the shit out of Dekes, which according to witnesses never happened.

"Have a seat, Penny," she announced taking her own chair behind the large desk. Penny sat down looking up at the large portrait of Pope Pius the XII on the wall behind her desk surrounded by rows of framed black and white pictures of Priests and Bishops. They all carried the same faint smile, an expression of blissful, mindless contentment as if they knew a fantastic spiritual secret unknown to anyone outside the Catholic Church.

To Penny, Catholicism was a mass of complicated rules and regulations having little to do with his everyday life. Not that he was against the organization or even the message that he tried to understand in Sunday service. They had treated him well, fed, clothed him, put a roof over his head, and provided his education. For that, he was grateful. He simply did not believe in praying for people who were already dead.

Though he hadn't attended much, the church in Kansas had been bedrock Baptist, a Bible-pounding, baptizing-in-the-river religion where people shouted, jumped, and praised God out loud. Here, the funeral-like Mass where worship in front of statues just seemed wrong and a far cry from what he had known before.

Sister Miller, a small woman, barely five feet tall, carried an air of control and inner strength that was impossible to ignore. Now well into her sixties, she had been a nun since eighteen. She spoke in a quiet, measured tone that both calmed the listener and held attention at the same time. Aside from her commanding demeanor, Penny was intrigued with the woman's pale blue eyes, the lightest colored eyes he had ever seen on anyone. As he sat watching her read a thick file, he wondered if anyone else found them as interesting as he did.

After a moment, she carefully removed her glasses and smiled. "I had just been reviewing your final grades before graduation - very commendable. You were able to challenge the senior exams and pass them all."

"Yes, Ma'am."

"I understand you do not want to participate in the graduation ceremony. Why is that?"

Penny thought for a moment. "Ma'am, I have someone coming to pick me up tomorrow."

Sister Miller smiled. "Don't you think that person would want to see you graduate?"

Penny felt like the room was getting warmer. "Ma'am, that person is my boss. He has no interest in anything other than getting me back up into the mountains." He fought to control the rising anger. There was no way he was not going to be standing on the curb with a packed bag tomorrow morning. It was all he had left and, god-damn-it, nobody was going to take it away. Not this. Not now.

As if reading his mind, Sister Miller leaned forward in her chair. "You've done what the State of Montana has asked you to do, Penny. It wouldn't be fair of me to ask you for more. Here," she said sliding the manila envelop toward him. He slowly opened it. The paper inside: a High School Diploma from the *Montana School for Boys, Missoula, Montana. 1940.* Awarded to Pendelton Dale Reynolds.

"Go start your life, Penny," she said softly. "Go find what you're looking for."

Six days later, at midnight on May 10, 1940, the German Army invaded France, Holland, and Belgium. For Penny... he would not be looking for long.

Chapter Fifteen

It had been an unusually hot week, especially for this early in the summer. The mid-eighties usually arrived around mid to late July. By then most of the scrub grass would have turned brown and the heavy pine needle thatch dried out from the winter snow, all conditions that made perfect tinder for the fires that always came later in the year.

The papers would later report that the fire that started up on Cole Cabin Ridge, Montana, just west of Lost Trail Pass that late afternoon in May was an event that no one could have prepared for. A fast moving storm had rolled into and over the jagged ridges of the Bitter Root Mountains from the Idaho side that morning, its blue-black storm clouds spreading across the horizon at thirty-miles-an-hour.

What was unusual was that the clouds held little to no moisture. What they did bring was a spread of thunderous lightning like nothing the area old timers had ever seen before. One of the few ranchers who witnessed the storm and would later survive the fire, reported to the local newspaper that he had been convinced that God was about to end the world with heaven's own lightning. In all his seventy-four years of living in the mountains he had never seen so many lightning strikes in such a short amount of time. He would later say that it "was like a massive line of giant canons firing one after another for thirty minutes. It scared the *BeJesus* out of me," he had said.

The first twenty-mile long lightning bolt strikes hit the tops of the old growth timber just below Lost Trail Ridge, setting a three-and-a-half-mile wide swath of prime Montana timber ablaze within seconds. The back side of the fast moving storm sent a four-mile-wide barrage of lightning into the Salmon River Flats two miles farther up the Bitter Root Valley and fifty miles east of Missoula. The high winds had taken over, and in less than thirty minutes, both fires joined on Cole Cabin Ridge in a towering wall of flames that could be seen ten miles away.

A month earlier…. on the fifth of May at nine o'clock sharp, Edwards, a man of his word, turned the corner of Lake Street in downtown Missoula to pick up a very relieved young man standing on the curb.

"That's a real nice suit ya' got there, sir," announced Edwards leaning over and opening the passenger side door of the truck. "Not sure how it's going to hold up in the woods. You ready to go?" he asked smiling.

Penny tossed his suitcase into the bed of the truck and quickly hopped in. "More than ready," he replied shaking hands while pulling off his tie. "Let's go." On the long drive back up to the station, Penny told Edwards all about his time at the home - the meals, the classes, and even the fight.

Edwards seemed to be greatly relieved that Penny's time spent there had not been a terrible experience. He had felt guilty for taking him there in the first place, and now hearing that he had not been scarred by his time at the home took a great weight off his shoulders. The last thing he had wanted to do was cause the kid any more pain than he had already endured.

As per Pearson's orders, for the next three weeks, Edwards put Penny, the youngest of the crew, under the supervision of Kelly Habner, a forty-year-old seasoned fire boss tasked to run the brand new training program, a program that had just been approved by the Forestry Department. Penny, along with fifteen other men, learned how to properly fell trees with a Collins axe, set back fires, dig fire breaks with short handled shovels, and run water lines from the new water trucks that had just been brought out from the East. The training was a grinding ordeal of twelve-hour days and short nights simulating what the rookies might encounter on a real burn.

On days when the woods were too wet to train in, class moved indoors where land navigation was taught, maps of the area were memorized, compass work was honed to a fine edge, and basic fire survival was instructed. Haber talked about canyon blowouts and fire tornados that exploded young pine trees by super heating the sap and then exploding like a bomb. He talked about how dangerous and fast moving grass fires were, that they were just as deadly as a full-blown tree fire.

As the days and nights rolled into each other, Penny felt himself getting stronger, tougher, and smarter. At the end of the third week of nearly nonstop training, the bleeding blisters from swinging an axe had turned into marble-hard callouses. The early leg soreness that had bothered him well into the night after running on mountain trails faded away. Now he could run all day carrying a forty-pound pack as if he had been doing it for years.

And yet, for all his training and new found knowledge, nothing could have prepared him for what he saw late in the afternoon on that unusually hot day in May. The fire station had been notified by the Lost Trail Fire Watch Tower that heavy white smoke was seen rolling out of the canyon just west of Cole Cabin Ridge. By the looks of it, something big was causing it.

Penny was on the first truck in the convoy of five as they raced down the newly laid gravel roadbed, a highway that had not been paved yet. From several miles away, they could see a huge towering cloud of smoke rising at least a thousand feet into the sky.

As the crew crested the bluff and got their first look at what was happening down on the valley floor below, they were shocked by the height and intensity of the flames a quarter mile away.

"Holy shit," announced Habner stopping the truck and staring out the windshield. "Those flames have got to be at least thirty feet high."

Penny looked over at the senior crew leader who seemed to have aged ten years. "Ah, what now? How do we put that out?"

Habner quickly opened the door of the truck and stepped out, still trying to comprehend the massive scope of the fire. He took his binoculars and scanned the valley below. "Penny, I have something I need you to do," he said still looking through the binoculars.

Penny grabbed his backpack and axe out of the back of the truck and stepped up beside the crew boss, working hard at keeping his rising fear under control. The rest of the team members were now pulling on their gear and getting ready to move.

Habner looked over at Penny, his face deeply etched with concern. "I need you to follow this small ridge and get down to that house and stock barn," he announced pointing to a large white house and red barn a quarter mile away. It would take us too long to drive down there by using the main road. I need you to get down there as fast as you can and see if old man Tyler is home. If he is, help him get his stock out of that barn."

He turned to the rest of the crew who were anxiously standing behind him. "The rest of you head down that draw over there and start digging a fire line. We're not going to be able to knock this down; it's too big. But maybe we can channel part of it towards the river. John, get back on the road and tell Pearson we need every swinging dick up here, anyone who can carry an axe, and both dozers as fast as they can get here."

Penny adjusted his pack waist strap still not sure if Habner was going to give him further instructions. The Crew boss looked over at him. "Jesus, boy, why are you still standing here?" he shouted. "Get moving! That fire is going to be on that place in no time. Move your ass!"

Jolted back into the moment, Penny turned, jumped off the edge of the road, and bounded down the knee high grassy hillside. Behind him he could hear the shouts and commands of Habner getting the firebreak crew moving.

In less than five minutes, Penny had run through the front gate of the house and jumped up the stairs onto the porch. "Hello!" he shouted, pounding on the door. "Anybody home?"

Penny tried seeing past the curtains as he pounded on the front window. "Hello! Anybody home?" he shouted knocking on the glass.

Deciding that no one was home, he jumped off the porch and headed to the barn. As he opened the wide stock gate he could hear the sound of the horses whinnying inside. He stepped up to the big double doors, stunned to see that they had been padlocked. 'Shit," he whispered, trying to think of what to do next. Running to the corner of the building, he could now see the flames and smoke in the deep grass less than a hundred yards away and moving fast.

With no time to spare, he ran back around to the front of the barn and with a single swing of his axe knocked the lock and hasp off the door. He jerked the doors wide and stepped inside. On the far left side, three horses paced and stamped in their stalls, intuitively sensing that real danger was moving closer.

Penny quickly opened all the stalls and shouted for the horses to leave. All three bolted and were out of sight in seconds. Just as he was about to leave, something moved off to his right. Pigs, there was a large sow and about ten piglets scurrying around in a straw-covered pen on the other side of the barn. He now smelled smoke. He ran over and opened the pen's gate, shouting and waving his arms.

Amazingly, the more he shouted and tried to herd the group, the more they simply ran around inside the pen and would not leave. Frustrated, he jumped over the stall and pushed open the second set of high barn doors. Instantly a heavy blast of thick smoke and heat blew through the doorway nearly knocking him down. The four-rail fence surrounding the barn was now on fire.

Trying to not suck in any more smoke, he ran back to the front doors of the barn, deciding that the pigs were on their own. He jumped back up to the porch, wanting to make sure one last time that nobody was home before he headed back up the ridge. "Hello!" he shouted pounding on the door. "Any body here?"

Just as he turned to leave, his heart dropped, hearing the faint reply of "Hold on" coming from inside.

Penny went back to the door and then looked back in the big front window. "Hey, who's there?" he shouted.

The front door suddenly opened. "What the hell is going on?" commanded the old man on crutches, trying to steady himself in the doorway. "I got a busted ankle. Was taking a nap. Who the hell are you?"

Before Penny could answer, the roaring sound of the barn suddenly catching fire answered the question. Having both doors opened at each end had turned the structure into a flaming wind tunnel.

"Jesus Christ!" shouted the old man hobbling out onto the porch, "My barn... my horses! We got to get them out."

Penny grabbed his arm. "I already let them out. C'mon, we have to go!" he shouted, feeling the heat from the now fully engulfed barn.

The old man jerked his arm away. "No. My papers are in the house. Got to get my papers. He pushed past Penny and disappeared inside. The heavy smoke and heat from the barn was now blowing across the porch making it impossible to see the front yard. Not knowing what else to do, Penny ran into the house looking for the old man, as thick black smoke began rolling in waves just under the ceiling inside. The house was now on fire.

Choking on the smoke, Penny ran back into the back bedroom and found the old man on his hands and knees coughing and gagging. Staying low, he grabbed the man by the back of his shirt collar and began dragging him out of the room as the heat and smoke grew more intense.

With all the strength he had left, he pulled the man across the living room floor and out onto the front porch, falling to his knees, gasping for air.

Just as he was about to pass out, somebody jerked him to his feet and half running dragged him across the front yard. Penny looked over and saw that Habner was the force holding him up. "C'mon, kid!" he shouted. "We gotta run for it. Move it!" Slowly, Penny's head cleared, and in minutes he, along with Habner and two other members of the crew, reached the top of the small ridge and the roadbed.

On the fire line, when the smoke is thick and the trees are nothing more than giant exploding torches, time is compressed, distorted, measured in what the fire does, where it goes, and what it kills. Veterans, men who have been in the woods on big burns in the past, tell rookies that once they see the real face of the beast, they can never be the same. A man cannot get that close to a bad death and then walk away without getting a scar. Nothing that valuable was ever free. For Penny, the baptism of fire only solidified in his mind that this was what he really needed to do... what he was meant to do.

After the last ember died out six days later and the damage assessed, in all ten homes, six barns, and forty-seven square miles of Montana timber had burned to a grey ash. The only thing that saved the small town of Darby, a town of three hundred souls farther down the valley, had been a major wind change and a nearly Biblical rainstorm that stopped the advance on the last day. Fortunately, there had only been one fatality, eighty-two-year-old Jessup Tyler, the man Penny had tried to save. He had never made it off his front porch. He had died in the house he was born in.

Chapter Sixteen

"Sir, are you sure this is where you want to go? I mean... New Jersey?"

Colonel Lee had expected skepticism concerning his decisions for the Airborne Program. He sat back in his chair, smiling, enjoying the young Captain's confusion. He and his staff had only been in Camp Claiborne, Louisiana, for two weeks but they were already turning conventional military wisdom on its head. The idea of training and putting large numbers of Airborne Infantry onto a hostile objective had been more of an amusing proposal in the United States military than anything else until now. The gray-beards who filled the senior ranks within the Department of the Army and who scuttled along the halls of Washington, D.C. considered the idea of soldiers jumping out of perfectly good airplanes in enough numbers to turn the tide of any battle pure folly.

"That's exactly where I want to go, Tim," replied Lee. "The two hundred foot towers are still there from the World's Fair, towers that we can use in the training program. It's perfect."

Lee, a forty-six-year-old career Army officer from Dunn, North Carolina, had served in the Great War with the American Expeditionary Force in France and was now the newly designated Commander of the fledgling Airborne Parachute Platoon, a unit signed into existence by President

Roosevelt that year, a unit that would eventually change the course of history.

The German military had already perfected the use of Airborne troops during the invasion of Holland in May of 1940 and the rest of the world had taken notice. Colonel Lee had been given a direct Department of the Army mandate to start, train, and equip a Parachute unit on par with the German Army(Fallschirmjäger.) In reality, the German Paratroops had actually been attached to the Luftwaffe due to the aircraft platform used for jumping, cold comfort for the people of Holland who felt the full sledgehammer force of the German paratroopers landing on their soil.

Every line officer on active duty, including Colonel Lee, knew that it was only a matter of months, if not weeks, before the United States entered the war. Germany had unleashed a massive military machine on its European neighbors in the early fall of 1939 in a quest for total domination and world control. Within the walls of the American government, the men who made the hard decisions knew in their hearts that it would be impossible to *not* enter the war in the near future.

The fires of World War had been lit, fires that would not be put out for four long years. When the smoke finally cleared and the damage assessed, over sixty million people would be dead.

Lee rummaged through a stack of papers on his desk. "Ah, here it is. This is a press clipping from the Daily Missoulian out of Missoula, Montana - God's country. It talks about a group of fire fighters up in some place called Sealy Lake." He handed the clipping to the Captain. "Take a look at it. You'll see why I am interested."

The young officer took a seat on the other side of the desk and slowly read the article.

Daring or daft

By Harold Pressman

August 17, 1940

Last year a new idea began circulating about an innovative way to fight the annual bout of destructive forest fires that plague the region. The newly formed Department of Forestry has been testing the idea of dropping firemen by parachute into remote areas in and around forest fires.

Currently there are seven brave souls that have taken up the challenge and are training at the Sealy Lake Ranger Station eighty-miles northeast of Missoula. These men call themselves "Smoke Jumpers" and are dedicated to the novel concept of jumping out of airplanes to fight forest fires.

Mitch Edwards, the program coordinator, who has already made twelve jumps, says: "The concept is sound. Jumping within an hour into areas that would normally take a ground crew a day to get to is the best way to get small fires under control before they become too big to handle."

When Mister Edwards was asked about what kind of man it takes to become a Smoke Jumper, his reply was:"It takes someone with great physical stamina and training in firefighting techniques. We have a range of ages from 35 to our youngest jumper at 18."

According to Edwards, the program hopes to expand and spread to other locations such as Canada where Smoke Jumping has caught the attention of the Canadian Government.

In this reporter's opinion, I do believe that best intentions are present but that logic and common sense may have taken a back seat to hubris. Only the future will tell if this is daring or just plain daft.

The officer looked up from his reading. "Sir, I am not sure what you want?"

Lee lit a cigarette and tossed the match into the large glass ashtray. What I want, Captain, is for you to manifest yourself on a plane and get up to Sealy Lake, Montana. I want you to tell Mister Edwards that his country has a need of his services. And while you're there, make contact with this eighteen-year-old kid that's going through the training. He's the age of the folks we will probably be training in the very near future. I want to see how he is reacting to the program, see if we can learn any lessons."

The officer stood up, still not sure of his orders. "Sir, just what exactly do you want me to do with these civilians? I mean, how hard do you want me to press this?"

Lee blew a lung full of smoke to the ceiling before answering. "Captain, the President of the United States wants an Airborne Program put together as quickly as possible. I want an Airborne Program even quicker. Right now, there is a man in Sealy Lake, Montana, doing the very thing the President has mandated. Your orders are to get up there, find out who these people report to, make contact, and bring them here under a standard consultant contract.

Before we start this operation, I need to see what's already being done. If we don't have to reinvent the wheel, it will be all the better. You are authorized to use whatever expenditures you see fit in accomplishing your mission. Money is not a concern. Are we clear on what I need done?"

"Yes, sir," replied the officer. "Right away, sir."

Lee picked up the desk phone. "I'm going to contact the base paymaster for financial allocations. Just keep your receipts."

"Yes, sir."

"That's all, Tim. Go find Mister Edwards. I need you wheels-up by tomorrow morning. Notify me when you get there. And, Tim...."

"Sir?"

Lee smiled while snuffing out his cigarette. "This is something our military has not done before. We're making history, and you're a part of it."

"Yes, sir."

****

Two thousand miles northwest, Penny stood in the windy open cargo door of the DC-3 as it leveled off at 2,500 feet. He tugged on the static line that was attached to the cable running the length of the fuselage just to be sure it was secure, a shiver running up his spine that had nothing to do with the cold.

Edwards stepped up close and shouted over the wind noise. "Remember your instructions. Stay tucked with your hands over the reserve handle. Bicycle out of any line twists and be facing the wind when you land. Okay?"

Penny nodded and gave a thumbs-up as he felt the plane slow and then drop under his feet. Everything they had done up to now: three weeks of ground parachute training, countless practice jumps and falls off the back of a moving pickup truck, hours of classroom work on rigging packing and then repacking had all come down to the next ten seconds.

More out of nervousness than anything else, Penny tugged on his football helmet's chinstrap one more time just to be sure it was tight. He trusted the A7 parachute on his back, a parachute he had packed himself under Edwards' watchful eye. He trusted the reserve on his chest. But most of all, he trusted Mitch Edwards, a man who had almost become a second father. If Mitch had enough confidence in him to give him this chance, then, by God, that was enough. Despite his fear, he was not about to let him down.

As Mitch grabbed his elbow moving him close to the door, Penny tried to imagine what his father would think of him now. Christ, what would his mother think about all this?

"Stand by!" shouted Edwards, giving him a thumbs-up. As the plane slowed even further, Penny suddenly felt as if he had drifted out of his body and was now standing a short distance away watching everything unfold. Time seemed to stop. Even the sound of the wind and the engine noise had all but disappeared as he focused on the sound of his own breathing.

He took a final deep breath. He was calm, strangely relaxed, as he felt Edwards slap him on the shoulder and shout "Go!"

Without hesitation, he stepped out into the howling wind and was changed forever. Pendleton Charles Reynolds, a seventeen-and-a-half-year-old Smoke Jumper candidate from 'nowhere,' Kansas, just made his first parachute jump. What would his mother think indeed?

Chapter Seventeen

It took two solid kicks to get the door open. The only thing that Hans and his unit had been doing since moving into the city of Arnhem had been knocking down doors and searching the Dutch homes for weapons. It had been only five days since the invasion, and buildings throughout the city still smoldered.

Surprisingly, the Royal Dutch Army had put up more resistance than anyone within the German command had expected. The invasion had started on the 10th of May and had ended on the 15th but the tiny Dutch Army had been no match for the German war machine.The German Luftwaffe and Army had turned half of the city of Rotterdam and almost every other Holland town and village into rubble. Over four thousand civilians and two thousand Royal Dutch Army soldiers had been killed in the five-day period. The amount of damage on the small country and its population had been immense and had ended with a deeply despondent Dutch forces' Commander in Chief, General Henri Winkelman, personally signing surrender documents.

The SS had been dispersed throughout Holland with a directive to seize all weapons in the hands of the population and to ferret out any Dutch resistance forces still active. Even after the Government's official surrender in Rotterdam a week earlier, German soldiers were still dying at the hands of sporadic snipers and civilian insurgents. He had lost track of the number of homes he and his unit had been through, recovering hundreds of weapons and executing over forty insurgents in the process. In Hans' mind, the Dutch were a defeated people. The sooner they recognized it and fell in line, the better off their lives would be. For the most part, the civilian population had been compliant and the ones who hadn't, had paid a heavy price in blood.

The part of the mission that Hans enjoyed most was that of serving as judge, jury, and executioner when Dutch resistance fighters were found. There were no trials, no judicial arguments, and no concessions for the fighter, man or woman, only a swift walk to a wall followed by a bullet through the forehead.

In Hans' mind, this was the way wars should be fought - the enemy destroyed. The fuzzy headed political mentality resulting in German surrender and appeasement following the Great War was over. Now, crushing the enemy without mercy was the only way to win, and he was more than willing to be the instrument of that message delivery.

He had been experimenting over the last week. He had studied the efficiency of each of his weapons up close. The MP40 machinegun fired a fairly light 9mm slug that tended to shoot high and to the left, and it was full-auto which tended to put more rounds into the body than was needed to kill a person. His rifle, on the other hand, fired the standard Mauser 7.57 x 92 round, a much heavier slug that hit with sledgehammer force at close range. In the last three days he had been shooting most of the people they came across with it from around 20 yards. He had been able to deliver precise head shots with the rifle from a greater distance in comparison, something not easy to do with the P40.

He found it interesting that most of the resistance fighters and Dutch Army holdouts remained oddly stoic as they were led to their deaths. Of course there had been a few who had begged and pleaded not to be shot over the last few days, some speaking perfect German, an unsettling discovery. Some had invoked ties to family and children while others had proclaimed the terrible injustice of it all. Some had claimed that they had money, gold, or jewels to trade for their lives. A few women had offered themselves in exchange for life and several times half the squad had indulged, one after another, but when it was over each time the woman had still been shot. Nothing any of them had said or done could have saved them... nothing.

There really wasn't anything in particular that he had against the Dutch, other than the fact that they seemed overly sentimental about life. But for Hans, the more someone cried, wailed, or pissed themselves, the more he wanted them to die. He hated to see that pathetic blubbering weakness. To him it was a fatal flaw in character.

At times he had made the killings more palatable by doing things to amuse the rest of his squad. One of the older resistance fighters found hiding in a basement on the outskirts of town had started to plead for mercy as he was stood against a wall near the Oosterbeek Bridge. He had pulled several pictures out of his wallet, pictures of his wife and young son, shouting and crying that he had a family that needed him and that he did not deserve to die in this way. After several minutes of listening to the begging and sobbing, Hans had told the man that if he could eat the pictures and sing the Dutch National Anthem at the same time, he would let him live. Sergeant Dietz, exhausted from the heat of the day, had walked over and taken a seat on the hood of a burned-out car while lighting a cigarette, showing only mild interest in the small drama Hans had started. The private had been killing people all day. What would be the point of stopping him now?

The terrified resistance fighter had quickly torn up the pictures of his family, stuffed them into his mouth, and chokingly begun to sing *Het Whilimus*, tears of desperate hope rolling down his face. As the rest of his squad stood and laughed, Hans had raised his P40 and shot the man to pieces.

Walking away from the murder, he had wondered how he would he act in the face of imminent death? How would he spend the last seconds of his life - pleading, crying for more minutes to live, taking one more look at the sky? How much was that worth? What would he be willing to pay?

Hans walked down the road, the smoke of several burning buildings wafting by as he loaded a fresh magazine into his P40, willfully dismissing the life and death introspection. He had more important things to think about. Pondering his own death was not one of them.

There was a rumor, and it was probably just a rumor, that they would be getting a hot meal today from one of the Army's mobile kitchens, something they had not had in a week. In Hans' way of thinking, going without decent food this long was the real deprivation. Killing some sniveling Dutchman was more of an inconvenience than anything else. At times like this, he thought, repositioning the rifle sling on his shoulder, a man needed to keep his priorities straight. Who knew what could happen if he started second-guessing himself.

****

It had been a week since Penny had made his first jump, and now he stood in the door of the same DC-3 waiting for Edwards to give him the "go" for his second jump. This time he was not alone. Three more members of his class now stood nervously behind him waiting for the "go" command.

"Stand by!" shouted Edwards, standing by the door, the cold Montana wind whipping at his clothing. He motioned for Penny to step forward to the jump side. The engine slowed and the plane leveled off. Edwards grabbed the two metal handles on the inside of the door and leaned out. Penny tugged on the clipped-in static line once more as Edwards pulled himself back in the aircraft and then pointing to Penny shouted "Go!"

Immediately, Penny took a short step and then hopped out into the howling slipstream, feeling the parachute and then the suspension lines rip out of the deployment bag on his back. He was under canopy in seconds.

For Penny, it was amazing how the noise level of the aircraft and the wind rush of the door almost immediately went quiet when he was under canopy, the only sound - the creak of his harness and the sound of his own breathing. Fifteen hundred feet below his boots, he could see the cleared drop zone ringed by an expansive dark green border of pine trees and tall meadow grass. The view from this height of the Montana landscape was incredible.

Looking past his feet, he twisted in the harness, looking for the bright orange windsock that marked wind direction. Spotting it over his left shoulder, he grabbed high on the front left riser and pulled it down to his chest. Slowly, the canopy turned. He could now see the windsock straight ahead a thousand feet below. Scanning the ground, he spotted several cars and Pearson's truck pull to the edge of the drop zone as he continued to descend.

The ground was now coming up fast, and he bent his legs, pulled his feet and knees together, tucked his chin on his chest, and prepared for landing. Seconds later, he thudded to the ground, rolling onto his side, as the canopy and suspension lines drifted down to the ground around him. Overjoyed, he stood up and shouted, unable to hold back the adrenaline rush any longer. He could not stop smiling as he watched the other members of his class thud to the ground close by. Still shaking from the rush, he quickly started rolling up the suspension lines and pulling in armloads of billowing canopy.

Penny watched as a small group of men started walking across the field in his direction. Overhead, the DC-3 made a low pass, dipped its wings, and then disappeared over the eastern ridge. As the men grew closer, his thoughts raced back to that first night in the boxcar, hours after he had run away from home when he saw that one of the men appeared to be in a police uniform. But to his relief, as the men grew close, he could see that the man was wearing a dark brown jacket with shiny buttons and a light brown, almost pink pair of pants. He recognized the military uniform, like the ones he had seen in magazine pictures.

"Penny, that was great!" announced Pearson stepping up, smiling. He found Penny's hand in the tangle of suspension lines and shook it as the other jumpers walked up to the group.

"Fine job, gentlemen. Fine job!" continued Pearson shaking hands and patting the shoulders of the other jumpers.

"Captain, this is the young man I was telling you about," announced Pearson proudly pointing to Penny. "He is just about to turn eighteen and is the youngest member of our first Smoke Jumper class. Penny, I'd like you to meet Captain Tim Barns of the United States Army."

Still not sure what was going on, Penny stepped forward and shook hands with the smiling officer. "Captain, pleasure to meet you."

"Oh no, young man, the pleasure is all mine. That was very impressive, what you just did, very impressive indeed. You are without a doubt the youngest parachutist in the country. Amazing."

"Thank you, sir," replied Penny, embarrassed. "I have a good instructor."

The officer stepped close and patted him on the shoulder. "Well, son, that's why I am here. Let's head back to Mister Pearson's office. We have a lot to talk about, young man."

More than a little nervous, Penny looked over at Pearson as if to ask if he was in some kind of trouble.

As if reading his mind, Pearson smiled and then slapped him on the back. "C'mon, Penny. Relax. I think you're gonna find this very interesting."

Chapter Eighteen

As the DC-3 made its final approach into the Sealy Lake airstrip, Edwards sat down on the web bench across from the open cargo door watching the tall pines that ringed the perimeter of the strip grow taller as they descended.

He could not have been more proud of the men in the class, especially Penny, who over the last few months had gained twenty pounds of muscle and almost two inches in height. Even more impressive, the kid had proved fearless when it came to parachuting. It was amazing that someone that young could take to jumping so readily.

Edwards watched the dust from the strip kick up outside the door as the plane gently bounced once on landing and then settled to the ground as the engines throttled back with a roar. The plane made a quick turn at the end of the strip and then stopped with the engines winding down.

"Hey!" shouted the pilot looking back down the cabin where Edwards was sitting. "We done for the day? I'm gonna need to fuel pretty soon."

Edwards unbuckled the wide lap belt and stood up as the smell of warm engine exhaust filled the cabin. "Yeah, we're done," he replied walking forward. "You fellas are welcome to stay tonight. The cook is putting on a pretty good spread for the Army. Should be more than enough."

The pilot removed his headset and hung it on the hook by the sun visor. "Sounds good, Mitch. We'll chock up and be right in. I'm about to starve to death."

Two hours later, Penny, Edwards, Pearson, the Army Captain, and pilot sat around the large dining room table in the station drinking coffee and eating the last of the blackberry cobbler.

Penny was still trying to get his mind around the idea the Captain had shared. They wanted him and Mitch to go to some military base in Louisiana to help teach and organize a parachuting program for the United States Army, a new program that, according to Captain Barns, had been mandated by President Roosevelt himself.

"Penny, you haven't said much about what your parents might think about all of this," questioned Barns, lighting the cigar Edwards had just handed him.

An awkward silence filled the room. "Ah, Penny is an emancipated minor, Captain," announced Edwards. "Both of his parents are deceased."

Barns thought for a moment. "Jesus, son, I'm ah, I'm sorry to hear that. I, I did not know that."

Penny sat back in his chair surprised at how painful it was to bring up the subject of his parents. "It's all right," he said, trying to keep his voice from cracking. "I make my own decisions now, have been for a while." He looked over at Pearson who nodded and winked.

"I can see that," replied Barns. "Well now," he coughed trying to gather his thoughts. "Okay, well, here's what we would like to do. As I said, we are going to combine parts of the German Army's program currently being used with whatever information we get from you folks into a unit program that will fit our needs."

"Why do you need me?" asked Penny.

Barns smiled after blowing cigar smoke toward the ceiling. "Well because, Penny, most if not all of the men who will be taking this training will be close to your age. You're the demographic we are going to be putting into the program. By the way, when do you turn eighteen?"

"Three months from now."

"Perfect," replied Barns smiling. "I think the timeframes work out pretty well."

Edwards thought for a moment while sipping his coffee. "What do you mean by timeframes?" he asked, already knowing what Barns was getting at.

"Well, Penny will soon be eighteen and that is enlistment age."

"Enlistment?" questioned Pearson, surprised. "Who said anything about Penny enlisting in the Army?"

An incredulous smile crossed Barns' face. "Gentleman, surely you are aware of the coming storm. It is just a matter of time before the United States gets involved in the war in Europe."

"Aren't we kinda getting ahead of ourselves, there, Captain?" questioned Edwards. "Penny is an employee of the US Forest Service and a valuable member of the new Smoke Jumper program. I'm not really sure that going into the Army now is a smart thing to do. Course, he can speak for himself."

Barns shook his head. "Fellas, I hate to tell you this, but there is serious talk about the start of a peace time draft. In fact, a bill to get it all rolling has already made it through half of Congress."

"What's the draft?" questioned Penny, not sure if he was still the topic of conversation.

Edwards snuffed out his cigar. "It's when the government calls you into the service whether you want to go or not."

"They can do that?"

"Better believe it," replied Pearson. "When it comes to war, the government can pretty much do what it wants."

"You don't think the government has the right to ask its citizens to help defend it?" questioned Barns, trying hard not to sound too antagonistic. He had had this kind of conversation before with civilians and had learned to tread lightly.

Edwards leaned back in his chair, studying the young Captain. "I think it ought to be left up to me if I want to go to war or not. Seems kind of heavy handed to be forced to do it."

Barns smiled. "I see your point, Mitch. I'm just letting you know that the draft is probably going to be law soon and our young friend here is most likely going to be at the top of the list. Eighteen to thirty-five-year-olds will be called up. Ah, just curious, Mitch, how old are you?"

Edwards thought for a moment, trying to decide if Barns was making a direct challenge or not. "Turned thirty-six last May," he replied, taking a sip of his coffee.

Barns smiled faintly. "Well then, looks like you have nothing to worry about."

Sensing the tension in the room, Pearson spoke up. "Okay then, I guess we will cross that bridge when we get there. Gentleman, I have a twelve-year-old bottle of Scotch in the other room and I think we need to have some of it. Shall we?"

"Sounds good to me," replied Barns. "How about having it out on the front porch? I'd like to see this *Big Sky* everyone is talking about at night."

As the group slowly shuffled onto the front porch into the cool night, a definable unease hung in the air. A hard truth had been released, a truth they had all sensed but had not verbalized, at least not in a manner that could involve those they knew. War was coming and with it, massive changes to the lives they were now living. They all knew it. Nobody was going to be able to sit this one out.

Pearson poured a bit of Scotch into each man's glass as they sat on the porch. "Gentleman, an Irish toast, if I may?" he announced raising his glass. "To the shores of Ireland and to all the men that God made mad, where all their wars are merry and all their songs are sad. Cheers."

Penny downed the shot in one gulp and immediately regretted it. The Scotch burned a fiery path down his throat, stealing his breath and making him cough, both at the same time. The other men roared in laughter as Penny coughed and wheezed.

"Nothing like a virgin's first roll in the hay," laughed Edwards patting Penny on the back.

Pearson walked over and poured Penny another shot. "Here you go, slugger. The second one is always better."

Penny wiped the tears out of his eyes still trying to catch his breath. *How could these guys drink this stuff,* he thought holding the glass away from his face as if it were on fire. Watching the group drink down a second shot, he held his nose and quickly drained his glass. Pearson had lied. The second one hurt and burned just as bad as the first. Another round of coughing and wheezing led to loud laughter from the group.

For all the misery the Scotch brought, Penny had never enjoyed himself more. He was being treated like an equal, not some kid that needed a handout or to be watched over, but like a man who had something to offer.

Far above, the cold dark Montana sky filled with millions of tiny white jewels was a silent witness to the past, present, and the undecided future. From east to west, a shooting star flashed by, unseen by the jovial crowd below, a metaphor for the speed of light changes that were on the way - changes beyond comprehension.

Chapter Nineteen

Three weeks after they had rolled into Holland, new orders had come from Himmler that the entire Tenth SS Division was being sent to France. The push to solidify the Western front needed to be achieved before winter so now every combat unit close to the area of advance would be put into the fight.

As a bit of irony, at least in Hans' mind, he had just been promoted to Corporal. Evidently he had gained a reputation for his ruthless and pervasive lack of mercy in dealing with the enemy or anyone else who stood in the way of his mission. People in authority were starting to notice. Dietz had put him in for the rank, and the promotion had been approved at the Commander's level.

When Hans thought about it, he was only doing what any loyal and dedicated SS man should do. This was his war and he refused to fight it on any other terms than his own. The treaties and misguided agreements that settled the last war had not only crippled Germany economically for a generation but had crippled the German soul. In Hans' mind the German leadership had sold out at the end of the war, given in before the contest had been decided. Whole Divisions of fully-armed and battle-tested men had suddenly been told to lay down their weapons, climb out of their trenches, and surrender. The war was over.

But as bad as the emotional wounds of surrender were on the German military, they were even worse on the collective mindset of the civilian population. In December of 1918, a month after the November Armistice had been signed, suicides within the German population had skyrocketed to horrendous levels.

Albert Gritzenburg, noted German playwright, poet, and survivor of the Western Front, wrote not long after the war: *"The collective darkness of mood and the terrible, unrelenting burden of defeat, have stabbed deep into the once vibrant heart of the German soul, possibly an unrecoverable injury."*

Hitler, in all his rage, had captured every bit of the pain and anger that festered in the country and had given it a voice, a voice that galvanized the German people into a staggering display of loyalty and action. That action, fueled by a need for revenge, was now moving across Europe at lightning speed, hence the term "Blitzkrieg" or Lightning war.

In Hans' mind and solid in the minds of the rest of the men in his unit, a great debt in blood was owed for a collective wrong. In the thinking of the German Military High Command this was a holy war, a war with those who had humiliated and crushed the German spirit, a wrong that would now be corrected without mercy.

"So, how heavy is the rank on your shoulders now, Corporal?" asked Dietz, jumping down from the back of the truck.

Hans cocked the bolt on his machinegun. "So far so good. Where are we anyway?" He handed Dietz a cigarette and then lit it. "Thanks for the promotion. Not sure I deserve it."

Dietz smiled, "You think this is about what you deserve?"

Hans lit his cigarette, not sure where Dietz was going with this. Every time he talked to the man he seemed to know him less. He had a way of looking at you that made you think he knew a terrible secret, something that would do you harm if he chose to divulge it.

Hans didn't answer the question as Dietz pulled a map out of his tunic pocket and waved for the rest of the squad to gather around. "Over here, ladies," he announced. As the rest of the platoon walked over, he opened the map and spread it on the back of the truck bed. "Okay, we are here." He pointed to a small red circle on the map. "This shithole of a town is called Amiens. It's just up ahead. Our job is to clear it, confiscate weapons, and capture any members of the French resistance. I want this place turned upside down. I want all the rats found. Are we clear?"

The men in the group nodded, they knew exactly what needed to be done - the same actions they had taken in Poland, Belgium, and Holland. It was going to be a long and terrible day for the people of Amiens.

The rules of engagement had not changed since Poland. "I want all radios on channel two and the CP set up later today. Not sure where that's going to be yet," continued Dietz. "Hans, take first and second squad and advance here on the west side. Stop your advance on the stream that runs on the backside of the village here. Questions?" None of the men spoke up. They were already loading weapons and adjusting gear.

"Mueller, take third and fourth squad and take the east side of the village. We should have Panzer support by noon although you know the bastards are never on time. Captain Volkmann wants this town secured by dark. I told him that would not be a problem."

He folded the map and tucked it back into his coat pocket just as a sudden shot fired by a sniper zipped through his head, blowing off the back of his skull. He was dead before he hit the street. Stunned by the attack, the rest of the platoon scattered into the ditches along the road as a second shot dropped another SS soldier crouched behind the truck not far from Dietz's body.

The survivors, now down in the weeds on both sides of the road, opened up with heavy rifle and machinegun fire. Green and red tracers ripped the wood line and thick undergrowth in a blind attempt to hit the sniper or anyone else who might be laying in ambush. It was amazing how much fire power two MG-42 machineguns could produce.

"Mueller, move up!" shouted Hans above the noise. "Take the right side of the road. We'll take the left. Sniper has high ground."

It took two more hours of maneuvering in and around the village, with three more men from Hans' platoon wounded before the sniper was located on a small rise shrouded in brush just inside the wood-line west of the village.

As Hans approached the sniper's body that had finally been cut down by flanking machinegun fire, he was surprised to see that it was a kid, maybe seventeen years old at the most though it was hard to tell from all the blood caused by the shot in the face and neck. The weapon laying nearby was a newer MAS 36, a standard French army bolt-action rifle fitted with a low power English scope, a setup that allowed him to kill Sargent Dietz and the other solider with hundred-yard head shots. Good shooting for a civilian, especially for someone this young.

Mueller walked over to Hans and the rest of the platoon that had gathered near the body. "What are your orders?"

he asked lighting a cigarette, fighting a slight hand tremor from adrenalin. He was another one of the older men who had transferred to the SS from the regular Army just before the Poland operation. In the six months they had served together this was only the second time they had spoken to one another.

"Why are you asking me?" replied Hans scanning the village a hundred yards away with his binoculars. "You have been a Corporal longer than me. What are *your* orders?"

Mueller blew out a full lungful of smoke, trying to let the nicotine calm his nerves. He had been the one who had killed the sniper when he flanked his position. "That may be true but Dietz wanted you to continue on in case he got himself killed," he replied before taking a long drink from his canteen. "He had you marked for leadership."

"And you know this how?" questioned Hans.

Mueller looked back down the road where Dietz's body still lay in blood and brains. "Because he told me so, just before we came here. I swear it. Said he was going to move you up the line at the end of the war. Liked the way you handled yourself. Besides, the nearest senior NCO is with the Panzers and God only knows when they will get here." He reloaded his P40 with a fresh magazine. "If we are going to clear the town, we need to do it before dark. There's no telling who else is down there with a rifle."

Hans thought for a moment and then walked over to the body and picked up the sniper rifle. He cared nothing for rank or position. In his opinion, most of the men he knew who carried authority were weak malingers or blowhards, people he went to great lengths to avoid. His motivation for being in the SS in the first place was not for personal gain but to enact vengeance on Germany's enemies. Now, the only thing going through his mind was how much blood would be taken out of the village of Amiens for the death of Sergeant Dietz. If the other men in his Platoon wanted him to lead that bit of justice, then so be it.

"All right. Here's what we are going to do," he announced pulling the sniper rifle sling over his shoulder. "Drag this piece of shit down to the road. Tie his feet to the back of the truck after you load up Dietz and the other one."

Mueller flicked his cigarette butt at the dead boy's head. "Then what?" he asked.

Hans started walking down the hill towards the road. "Then we clear the goddamned village just like Dietz said!" he shouted over his shoulder. "Let's go!" As if the gods of war themselves had heard the command, a low rumble of thunder rolled across the greying French sky in response.

Goddamned indeed, thought Mueller dragging the boy's body by the arm. Hell was on the way to Amiens and there was nothing they could do to stop it.

Chapter Twenty

Six days after drinking his first shot of Scotch at the Sealy Lake Ranger Station, Penny, along with Edwards and Captain Barns hopped down from the parked US Army DC-3 at Camp Pollock, Louisiana's newly laid airstrip twenty minutes away by car from Camp Claiborne. Since 1938 there had been a massive military infrastructure build-up in the south. Camp Pollock airfield was just the latest asset to be put in operation. They had landed just after noon on their way to a scheduled meeting with Colonel Lee at two o'clock that afternoon.

While Captain Barns was still at Sealy Lake, Pearson had been contacted by the highest authority within the Department of Forestry and had received the mandate to comply and assist Captain Barns with whatever plans and operational assistance he required. Understanding that there was heavy Government juice behind the order, Edwards and Penny had packed their bags, jumped a Government DC-3 in Missoula, and within days had flown down to Camp Pollock, Louisiana.

As they drove through the Camp Claiborne's main gate, Penny still found it hard to believe how his life had changed since the day of his father's funeral. Everything was new - the people, the landscape and, most importantly, the mind-numbing opportunity that lay ahead. He had two parachute jumps under his belt and, according to Edwards, he was now one of the most experienced parachutists in the United

States, an amazing feat accomplished before his eighteenth birthday.

The white-helmeted MP waved them through and after several minutes they parked in front of one of the single story green and white Operational and Headquarter buildings in Colonel Lee's command - Third Army, 34th Infantry Division.

As they stepped inside the building, a skinny soldier not much older than Penny greeted them from behind a desk by the door. He stood up as Captain Barns walked in. "Afternoon, sir. Colonel Lee is expecting you. And, sir, I need the two civilians to sign in please."

Barns took the clip board from the soldier and handed it to Edwards. "Just sign your name, fellas. It's routine."

Penny signed the sheet. No one had ever asked him to sign his name before. It made him feel oddly important. He handed the clipboard back.

"Right this way, gentlemen," announced the young man, "The Colonel is expecting you."

They walked down a short hallway stopping as the young aid knocked on door of the office at the end. Penny had never seen a building so clean before in his entire life. The dark brown wood floors had been buffed to a high shine. The pale green colored walls looked as if they had been painted that day. The room carried an antiseptic smell of a strong detergent or cleaner, close to what you would find in a hospital.

"Come in," replied a voice from inside the office.

As they entered, a man who appeared to be in his mid-forties, sat behind his desk, dressed in a crisp tan uniform.

He had a hawkish nose framed with deep set eyes and dark hair, giving him the appearance of a bird of prey.

"Gentlemen, come in," he announced smiling. He stood up and walked around the desk to shake hands with Edwards and then Penny. He nodded to Barns, "How was the trip out?"

"No problems, sir. Montana is truly a beautiful place."

"Yes, it is," replied Lee. "Always wanted to go fishing up on the Salmon River. Anyway fellas, it's Penny and Mitch, correct? Thank you for coming. I'm Colonel Lee if Captain Barns hadn't already told you. Have a seat. I'm in command of our little project."

He walked around his desk and sat down. "Corporal, why don't you see if you can get these fellas a couple of Coke-a-colas. It's hot out, and I know I could use one."

"Yes, sir," replied the aid.

"And get one for yourself," added the Colonel as the aid closed the office door behind him.

"All right, let's get to it," began Lee, opening a file on his desk. "First of all, thank you for coming down here even though we really did not leave you much choice. This program that we are getting ready to start is about to be mandated by the Secretary of the Army, who in turn gets his marching orders from the President of the United States - kind of an important chain of command."

As Penny sat and listened to the officer, he could not escape the surreal feeling of the meeting. Events seemed to be happening at a blinding speed, with new information, images, and emotions all rushing together to create a nearly overwhelming sense of disconnection. Intuitively, through the fog of it all, he knew deep in his gut that whatever was happening at this moment was going to be a major turning point in his life. After today nothing would be the same.

"Sir, this may sound like a dumb question," replied Edwards. "But how long do you think you're going to need us here?"

Lee sat back in his chair. "Well, this is what I was thinking. The Department of the Army has authorized the training of a full Platoon of soldiers in parachuting. They are going to be designated *Paratroopers*. The selection process has already started with men from some of our finest units. War is headed this way, gentlemen, and we need to be ready. It's not "if" it shows up; it's just a matter of "when". Mitch, what I would need specifically from you is a train-the-trainers kind of program with Penny your assistant. Put our boys through the same kind of program you have up in Montana. We are going to borrow some of the German Army Paratrooper protocols but it will mostly be your show till we get our folks up and running. You set the standards. The first group will be forty-eight willing souls - men who have volunteered to be part of this.

"Are we going to do this here, Colonel?" asked Edwards, trying to process what Lee was telling him.

Lee sat back in his chair and smiled, "Nope. I want to kick this off in New Jersey, in a place called Hightstown. The way I figure it, we need to be up and running in thirty days which gives you a timeframe for how long you need to be with us. I know that the timeline is short, but I have my orders."

Edwards thought for a moment. "Any particular reason you want the training in New Jersey, sir? And what about aircraft?"

Lee shuffled through the stack of papers on his desk. "Ah, here you go." He handed Edwards a newspaper with a large black and white photo on the front.

"What you're looking at there, Mitch, is the New York Worlds' Fair 250-foot parachute drop towers, a perfect parachuting simulator for what it would be like to hit the ground under an open canopy. There are also several empty hangers on the grounds for classroom and packing classes. As far as aircraft goes, you tell me what you need and it will be there."

Edwards handed the paper to Penny who studied the photo, trying to understand what he was looking at. Again the feeling of disconnection was overwhelming.

"Sounds interesting. What about our jobs back in Montana?" questioned Edwards. "A month is a long time away from my post. Hate to think I would lose it. I kinda like Montana."

"Same here, sir," announced Penny chiming in. It was the first time he had spoken since he sat down. Hearing Mitch say he did not want to lose his job put a bolt of fear through him. Montana was home. Just thinking about not having it was too terrible to ponder.

Seeing the alarm on Penny's face, Lee laughed. "No problem there, fellas. The Government of the United States is very grateful for your help with this program and I can assure you that your jobs will be waiting for you after we get this operation going. You have my word on it. Secondly, as a way of showing our appreciation for your service, we have provided a compensation package that should more than cover your stay with us." He slid two large manila envelopes across the desk. Penny's last name was on one of them.

"Mitch," continued Lee, "I understand that Penny here is a minor so his package is a little different than yours. We have assumed that he is legally under your adult supervision?"

Edwards looked over at Penny and put the thick envelope back on the desk. "Sir, with all due respect, Penny is an emancipated minor under Montana Law and is no longer considered a juvenile. Secondly, he is a paid member of the Sealy Lake fire crew, and Smoke Jumper - Class One. And most importantly of all, he gets paid the same amount of money I do or I am headed back to Montana tomorrow."

Lee thought for a moment and then looked over at Penny and smiled. "Well, young man, I want to apologize to you for not fully understanding the situation. Assumptions in the past on my part have always led to trouble. Sorry for not getting all the facts straight. Okay, Mitch," he said, easing back in his chair, "We will make it right. Do we have a deal?"

Edwards looked over at Penny and winked. "What do you think, partner?"

Penny thought for a moment and smiled. "Never been to New Jersey. Think I'd like to see it."

Edwards nodded to Lee. "All right then. You got a deal, Colonel."

At that very moment, that very second, Penny felt his life change. The cosmic shift was unmistakable.

Chapter Twenty-One

There had been no resistance as they moved into the village. The streets were empty as a pounding rain turned the cobblestone road into an inch-deep river. Hans' platoon moved through the gloom like quiet wraiths bristling with weapons and belts of glistening machinegun ammunition draped around their shoulders.

Soaked to the skin, the platoon broke into groups of twos and threes, spreading out over the town, taking stock - hunting. Behind the patrol, the troop truck crawled carrying the bodies of Dietz and the other SS man killed by the sniper. They laid side by side on their backs, unprotected from the rain, their blood running out of the bed and into the street in thin crimson streams.

Walking up to a small fountain in the village square, Hans laid the sniper rifle on the low stone wall that surrounded it. He motioned for Krieger, the young private carrying the radio. He doubted he would be able to contact the Panzers, supposedly in route, but he would give it a try.

Fucking rain, he thought taking the handset. "Lancer six, lancer six. This is Glass Dagger. Over."

The only reply was the static hiss. "Lancer six, Lancer six. Glass Dagger, Over." Again there was no reply. Frustrated, he tossed the headset back to Krieger as he spotted an older man across the courtyard carrying an enormous black umbrella walking his way. Hans motioned for the truck to drive up next to the fountain as the man approached.

"I,....I am George de Villier. I am the mayor of this,,,"

"I don't speak French," interrupted Hans as he stepped up close, reaching over and pulling the umbrella out of the man's hand and dropping it on the street. "Do you speak German?"

Hans locked a flat stare at the man not sure if he was trembling from the miserable rain or from barely controlled fear. Hans guessed the man to be in his middle sixties. His neatly trimmed beard and brown herringbone glasses gave him the appearance of a teacher or maybe a banker.

"I, I, speak a little German," replied the man nervously, his hand shaking as he wiped the rain droplets off his glasses.

Hans smiled without humor and pointed to the back of the large troop truck. "Go over there and tell me who that piece of shit is that's tied to the back of it. I want to know his name, and I want to know where he lives in this sewer. Go on. Move."

Slowly the man walked to the back of the truck as if a wild animal was tied to the bumper. Hans smiled as he watched the man vomit when he looked down at the body. From the look of it, he had had sausage, potatoes, and maybe some red wine for supper.

Trying to compose himself, the man wiped his mouth with a wet handkerchief and slowly walked back to where Hans was standing as a low peel of thunder rumbled in the distance.

"So, who is our friend and where does he live?" asked Hans in German.

"I am not sure but I think he is Maurice Valmont, Michael Valmont's oldest son. I think that's who it is, It's... it's, hard to tell from the blood and...."

"Very good," interrupted Hans. "Now where does this person live? Direct me to the house."

Hans could see a look of total dread cover the man's face as he desperately thought what he should say next. Wanting to make it easy for him, Hans suddenly shot the man in both legs, just below his knees, with a short burst from the P40. The rounds slammed into the man's shins, instantly punching small bits of pulpy flesh out the back of his calves. He dropped to the street in writhing agony, his cries and grunts of pain barely heard above the downpour.

Hans walked up and stood with his full weight on one of the man's shattered legs. "Where does he live?" he shouted as the man screamed.

"Tell me where he lives, and I will make the pain stop," he said, stepping off the man's leg.

"Third house on the left, on the left, just past the bakery," the man cried, pointing across the square. "The house with the blue shutters. My God, my legs, my legs...." he sobbed, trying to crawl away, the blood now flowing like tiny rivers behind him. Hans let him crawl another few feet before he calmly emptied the rest of the magazine into the Frenchman's lower back and buttocks.

"Go get everyone out of that house!" he shouted to several of the men in his platoon who had been standing by watching the killing. "The one with the blue shutters. Bring everyone here."

Krieger, the young radio operator suddenly walked up, pulling off his headset. "It's Volkmann," he announced excitedly. The comms are working." Hans took his helmet off and held the headset to his ear.

"Lancer six, lancer six. Glass Dagger. Over."

"Glass Dagger, we are inbound to your location."

Hans strained to hear the faint signal above the rain.

"Lancer Six, what is your ETA? Over."

The only thing he heard before the radio went dead was Captain Volkmann saying "22 hundred."

Irritated by the poor communication, he handed Keiger the headset as he watched two men being pushed and shoved by several members of Mueller's squad across the courtyard. They had been taken from the house with the blue shutters and were now headed his way. The older of the two walked with a pronounced limp, a man in his middle sixties. The other appeared to be in his late forties, close to his own father's age. With one last shove, the old man literally fell at Hans' feet. The younger man quickly bent down and helped him up, his face twisted in quiet rage. "Stop it!" he shouted to the soldier who had shoved him. "Can't you see he is disabled? My God!"

"Hey," announced Hans. "Pay attention to me, asshole. What is your name?"

The man turned and faced Hans, his face red with anger. "My name is Michael Valmont. This is my fa......"

"Enough!" interrupted Hans. "I don't speak French. Do either of you speak French?" he asked of the three soldiers who had brought the men.

"I do, Corporal," replied one of the soldiers.

"Good. Interpret," commanded Hans. "Ask him if he has a son. Ask him if the kid's name is Maurice Valmont?"

Before the soldier could speak, the older man spoke up in German. "Yes, he has a son. Maurice is my grandson."

"Ah, so you are Valmont Senior," replied Hans smiling, "the patriarch of the family."

"Yes. Where is my grandson? Is he safe?"

Hans nodded towards the truck behind him. "Oh, sorry to say old man, we killed him an hour ago. He shot two members of my platoon. He's tied to the back of the truck. Would you like to see him or maybe what is left of him?"

The old man's face instantly lost all color as a single tear rolled down his cheek.

"You see, Grandfather," continued Hans, "this is what happens to people who kill German soldiers."

Mueller!" commanded Hans, "String the kid up by his feet on that lamp post. He'll serve as an example."

"You cannot do this," replied the older Valmont alarmed. "It is inhuman. He is just a boy."

Hans turned and walked over to the fountain wall and picked up the sniper rifle. "That boy fired this and killed two German soldiers!" he shouted, dropping the rifle on the ground. "Where did he get the weapon?"

The old man stiffened. "The boy took the rifle without permission. It is mine," he said raising his chin in defiance. "I am a veteran of the Great War. I served under the greatest field commander ever to wear a uniform, *Major Jacques De*

Lamont, of the Fifth Fusiliers and I would be in this war if I had not been disabled in the Ardeans fighting you animals."

Hans laughed in surprise. "A true warrior, Grandfather? So what do you do now, old man? How do you channel your fighting spirit now that you are old and useless?"

Suddenly, with a desperate cry, the younger man tried to rush past Hans as he watched the body of his son being dragged by. "*Mon Die, mon fils*," he sobbed, dropping to his knees.

"You cannot do this!" shouted the old man. "It is against God. You cannot."

Hans raised the P40. "God has nothing to do with this," he replied softly, firing a full magazine into both men at point blank range. Their bodies jolted backwards in a spray of blood and bone.

Mueller, with the help of two other SS men, hoisted the body of the boy into the air on the arm of the lamppost with a section of commo wire.

"Drag these three off to the side of the road!" shouted Hans reloading his weapon. "Volkmann and the Panzers will be here at ten tonight. Mueller, get a machine gun in the bell tower of that church. The CP will be in there. Tell the rest of the platoon to get dry and eat. Stay in groups of three when they moving through the village. Move out."

Mueller nodded that he had heard as the rest of the platoon that had been standing nearby broke into small groups and moved farther into the village. The spectacle of jarring violence had emotionally drained the men who had witnessed it. They moved quietly off into the gloom like crippled wolves, unsure of their own involvement, ashamed of the kill.

For Hans there was no moral conundrum, no pang of remorse for his actions. In his way of thinking the boy was a resistance fighter and the father and grandfather were collaborators - pure and simple. He picked up the sniper rifle and broke it in half, smashing it against the fountain wall. The only thing he felt now was cold and wet as he looked over at the body of the boy gently swaying in the wind of the storm.

As he walked across the courtyard on his way to the church, he tried to imagine what his father would think of his leadership now. In the best of daydreams his father would smile and tell him how proud he was of him, maybe even pat his shoulder as a gesture of respect and kindness. Ah yes - the best daydreams.

Chapter Twenty-Two

Four days earlier it had taken them just under seven hours to fly the thirteen hundred miles from Camp Polk, Louisiana, to Hightstown, New Jersey, in the Army DC-3. Penny along with Edwards and ten other Army Paratrooper volunteers were the advance party for the first Airborne training platoon that would be headed up in the next few days. Colonel Lee had green-lighted the operation on direct orders from Washington and the cosmic wheels were turning. Edwards now had thirty-seven days.

For Edwards and the other soldiers in the plane, the seven hours flying time gave them a welcomed opportunity to sleep. For Penny, the excitement of the trip was nearly overwhelming. While the others lay sleeping sprawled on top of and in between the plane's cargo, Penny stayed fixed at one of the forward cabin windows not wanting to miss a minute of the journey. *How could anyone sleep through an adventure like this?*

They landed at the small municipal airport in Hightstown just after one in the afternoon as a light rain began to fall. As Penny jumped down from the open cargo door, he was surprised to see that the only building at the airstrip was a small refueling shed not much bigger than the one back home in Sealy Lake. The way Edwards had been talking about New Jersey and the New York area, you would have thought there would have been more to the place than this. So far he was not impressed. As far as he was concerned, it was going to be pretty hard for anything to beat the Bitterroot Mountains at sunrise.

Within an hour they had the plane unloaded, and with nothing else to do sat around talking and smoking cigarettes as they waited for the trucks to arrive. All the gear was to be taken to a large storage building that stood nearly at the foot of the two hundred foot towers about five miles from town, towers none of the men had seen before. Penny was far more leery of the towers than he was of jumping. Secretly, he was hoping that he would not have to mess with them since he had already completed Smoke Jumper training.

The trucks finally showed up a little after three. After a short ride they drove onto the compound. Penny was shocked, as were the rest of the men, the first time he saw the huge red metal structures. Two hundred feet did not sound like a great height, but when you stood next to an object that was two hundred feet tall, it was astonishingly high.

As the men walked around the base of the steel giants, there was a lot of nervous kidding around and loud bravado about who was going to shit their pants first on the ride up or down. Penny stayed quiet, knowing that the towers were a kid's carnival ride compared to standing in the open door of a DC-3 at 1500 feet, a slip stream going by at a hundred miles an hour doing everything it could to tear your head off the minute you stepped outside. That was when the real bowel movements started.

Four days had gone by since their arrival and the rain had not stopped, conditions that had not slowed or hindered the work at setting up the operation. By now the full complement of volunteers had arrived and were busy setting up cots, a small mess dining area, and, most importantly, five forty-foot-long parachute packing tables. It was incredible how big the building was, easily able to accommodate all fifty-four members of the cadre, pilots, and volunteers along with their gear. Penny was amazed at how fast everything had been put together.

Equally impressive were the three large palletized stacks of brand new A7 parachutes along with the newly designed 28-foot conical chest-mounted reserves with the B12 fasteners. All of the equipment appeared to be brand new but was of a surprising concern for Edwards when he examined the rigs more closely. He opened several containers and was shocked to discover that three of the rigs did not have the suspension lines actually attached to the risers. If they had been used, the men wearing them would have had a certain reserve ride or worse. On discovering the alarming discrepancy in the set ups, all one hundred and seven parachutes were unpacked, checked for proper assembly, and then repacked under Edwards' watchful eye by the men who would use them.

Staff Sergeant Brice Evans and Staff Sergeant Carl Beal had been chosen by Colonel Lee to be the lead trainers under Edwards and would be the first official "Jump Masters" initiated by the United States Army Paratrooper program. Both men were from Texas oddly enough and had been chosen from a volunteer pool of over a thousand applicants. Both were in peak physical condition and carried the quiet confidence and low-key manner that true leaders possessed.

Penny had become friends with the men, each wanting to know in great detail what it was like to jump from an airplane. They wanted to hear about what it was like to fight the forest fires in Montana. Edwards had told them about the Cole Cabin burn and Penny's part in it. All of the men in the unit were impressed by Penny's achievements at such a young age. He had their respect, not something easy to obtain from men almost twice his age.

Even though he only had two jumps, he enjoyed his status of having parachuting seniority. He liked being looked up to, flourishing in the aggressive male environment that was so much a part of the military.

Penny was confused that from the very beginning no one in the group had called him by his name but had permanently labeled him "Flash", not in a derogatory way or mocking term of derision, but one of respect like "Flash, what do you think about this?" or "Flash said we need to S fold the lines this way."

On the late afternoon of the fourth day, Penny finally asked Edwards why the men had been calling him Flash. Edwards laughed. "Well, I kinda let it slip just before we left that you got hit by lightning. Pretty funny, huh?"

Penny shook his head. "Hilarious. You know a nick name like that might end up sticking. Not sure how I feel about that."

Edwards laughed. "Sorry, Pard. I think the train has left the station on that one. Besides, it fits you, and how else are you going to explain how that fancy tattoo got on your back?" He patted Penny on the shoulder. "The guys think you're a stand-up Joe, Penny, one of them. That's a good thing. Trust me."

Penny thought for a moment. "I guess there are worse things to be called," he said smiling.

Edwards put his arm around Penny's shoulder as they walked to the mess area for supper. "Yes, my boy, there are. You have no idea."

Outside, the rain finally stopped, leaving a crisp clean smell in the air and gold shafts of setting sunlight shining through the clouds. For the men inside the hanger, events were happening thousands of miles away, things far beyond their control. A drama with a very hard edge and equally dark consequences was drawing them in. They were now on a path, a path that would lead to an inevitable rendezvous with destiny.

By eight o'clock the next morning the Platoon had already had breakfast and were just finishing up the two mile run followed by thirty minutes of grass drills, pushups, sit-ups, flutter kicks, and the infamous burpees, a four count ball-buster of an exercise that could make even the fittest paratrooper throw up or pass out if done long enough.

After grass drills the men went through PLF training, short for Parachute Landing Fall exercises. The platoon would line up behind large five-foot high wooden boxes and jump off, simulating landing under canopy. This drill emphasized a five points of contact routine that started with jumping off feet and knees together, landing on the balls of your feet, twisting right or left and trying to put the side of your calves on the ground, followed by the thigh and then the upper back in one smooth rolling motion.

Of course through all the instruction, Edwards used Penny as his demonstrator, making sure that every drill was done perfectly. After the demonstration Penny walked through the ranks of the platoon assisting those whose form was not yet up to snuff. By the end of the second week Edwards felt confident that the men were physically ready to move on to the actual Airborne section of the training, the tower drills and then the actual jumps. He had been meticulous at documenting the class protocols as were the two active duty

Jump Masters, who intuitively knew that they were setting up Airborne operations training for future Paratroopers.

Not only did he want the men to be ready physically for the rigors of jumping; he also wanted them to understand how the parachute worked and how it was packed. In later years the Parachute Riggers qualification would become a recognized MOS or Military Occupation Skill, a vital component within the Airborne community.

The morning of the tower drops, Edwards called Penny over from his work at the packing tables. "Hey, Pard, we are going to start dropping these guys in about an hour. If you would go ahead and jock up, I want them to see how it's done." He smiled when he saw the look of dread flash across Penny's face. "Something wrong?" he asked, enjoying himself.

Penny looked over at the men who were already getting suited up near the base of the tower. "Ah, no, you sure you want me to do it? I mean what about Evans and Beal?"

Edwards laughed and punched him on the shoulder, "C'mon tough guy, get your gear. You're up." He walked away smiling, knowing that the kid was about to face his fear that had bothered him from day one. He had seen the look of balls-deep concern in Penny's eyes the day they drove onto the compound.

Working hard at controlling his growing apprehension, Penny pulled one of the rigs off the stack and headed out to where the platoon was standing by the tower. Much to his embarrassment the group started cheering and clapping as he started walking across the expansive yard. As he walked into the middle of the group, Edwards pushed the electric hand control button lowering the cable and canopy hoop from the tower arm200 feet above. Sergeant Beal helped him into the A7 harness and had him walk away as he pulled the canopy and suspension lines out of the container.

As the steel 28-foot tower hoop settled five feet off the ground, Sergeant Evans attached the canopy's thick Apex ring to the cable release device. The rest of the men then draped the canopy around the ring and stood back. Sergeant Beal hooked in Penny's safety line and then looped it over the hoop. "When you get on top, Flash, and you're ready to go, unhook the safety line, let it drop, and then you'll be released. Got it?" he asked slapping Penny on the shoulder with a smile.

"Got it," he looked over at Edwards and gave him a thumbs up.

"All right. Just back up as I lift the ring. The cable will do all the work and you'll be held by your harness." He pushed the button and immediately the Hoop started to rise. Within minutes Penny was a hundred feet in the air. A minute later he reached the top and came to a heart-stopping jolt. With shaking hands, not bothering to sight see, he reached up, unclipped the safety line, and pulled it over the hoop, letting it drop past his feet to the waiting and cheering group below.

"Stand by!" shouted Edwards.

Penny gave a half-hearted thumbs-up, and before he could think of anything to shout back, he felt the gut-wrenching drop in the pit of his stomach as the cable released. "Holy shit!" he shouted, instinctively reaching up for the risers. It was amazing how fast the ground was coming up as he spotted the bright orange windsock below and to his left. He pulled down hard on the left riser, turning the canopy into the wind just before he thudded into the wet grass.

It wasn't a perfect PLF but he was down in one piece which was reward enough. He was now a jump-tower veteran. As he lay in the grass trying to catch his breath, a stab of deep melancholy touched his heart as he thought about his father and the incredible things like this that were going on without him. Shaking back an embarrassing tear, he sat up as several of the men came running up, laughing, congratulating him while helping him to his feet. Incredible things indeed.

Chapter Twenty-Three

Three days had passed since Hans' unit had entered the village of Miens. Their new orders now according to Volkmann were to stay put and wait for the rest of the Division to catch up. Half of the Tiger tanks assigned to the operation were currently bogged down up to their transfer wheels near the border, having become victims of the recent torrential rains that had turned the narrow dirt roads into knee-deep goo, slowing the heavy transports to a crawl.

Waiting for the rest of the unit to arrive, Hans and the remnant of his platoon spent their time patrolling the low hills and thick woods surrounding the village. Even though a curfew had been imposed, someone had taken the boy's body down from the lamppost along with the other men Hans had shot. Oddly enough, the bakery continued to produce bread even though the owners had been killed, a bit of strangeness nobody cared to explain.

When told of the brutal lesson Hans had given to the citizens of Miens for the killing of German soldiers, Captain Volkmann had been impressed by his decisive action. In his opinion, the French were a conquered people and needed hard correction in order to stay in line. Insurrection and resistance would be crushed, and if civilians were rolled up in that conflict, so be it. Volkmann had come from a long and influential lineage of Euro Prussian officers and government confidants, ultranationalists who had made fortunes and gained favors by having the right friends in high places. His dismissive tone and aristocratic air would normally have categorized him as some pretentious fop, but in reality he was a tough, pragmatic leader, fearless in battle and unconditionally supportive of the men in his command.

On the second day of the occupation, without fanfare or ceremony, members of Hans' unit buried Dietz and the other SS men in an unmarked patch of ground east of town. Hans had marked the coordinates on his map for reasons he still couldn't explain. Trying to think of Dietzhaving a family or even someone who really cared if he lived or died seemed unlikely. After going through his wallet and personal papers, Hans had been surprised to see that there had been no pictures of girlfriends, a wife, children, or any family letters for that matter... nothing. It appeared that the man had had no personal human contact with anyone other than those inside the SS community. Dropping him into an unmarked grave by the men he had served with was probably the only compassion and reverence he would get. Probably all he would have wanted.

Hans understood that sad nobility, that selfless dedication to a cause, a way of thinking that closed off every other channel of human emotion and connection. Men like Dietz were true believers, men who were capable of staggering levels of dedication, wounded souls who would do anything to maintain and promote their wonderfully dangerous view of the world, predators with conviction.

Hans poured a cup of hot tea as he sat in the church office, the current CP, late in the afternoon of the fourth day having just walked back into town from the latest patrol. Mueller was already asleep on the cot snoring softly, his wet muddy boots drying by the small fireplace in the far corner of the room. The priest who had lived in the room for years prior to the German's arrival had not been seen in days, another odd fact that no one in the village seemed to want to investigate.

The Captain had left earlier that morning, telling Hans that he was going to try and link up with the rest of the division still hours, maybe days, behind them. His orders were to hold the town at all cost. Hans' platoon was now the forward axis of advance for the entire Division. That morning just before Volkmann climbed into his half-track to leave, he tossed Hans a small plastic bag. "Congratulations," he announced climbing into the passenger side of the mud-spattered vehicle. "You did a good job here. I should be back before dark. Try not to get killed in the meantime." He smiled faintly and then nodded for his driver to go. Hans stepped back as the massive eight-ton KFZ 21 half-track lurched forward and then rumbled through the courtyard on its way out of town.

With the exhaust smoke from the track still hanging heavy in the air, Hans opened the bag and was shocked to see a brand new set of black and white SS collar tabs within the single white embroidered box, a box that designated him as SS Unterscharfuer. He had just been promoted to Sergeant.

***

Penny tugged on the overhead static-line clip, more out of nervousness than anything else. Standing in the open door of the DC-3 was familiar ground for him, as 1800 feet below the lush green New Jersey landscape rolled slowly by. Edwards grabbed the inside door frame and leaned out, the slipstream whipping the legs of his kaki jump suit. The weather could not have been better for jumping; a light three knot wind was blowing out of the west and the temperature was a pleasant sixty-three degrees. It was a perfect day to see if the training had been successful. Even though the skies were slightly overcast, rain was not in the forecast.

"Thirty seconds!" shouted Edwards after pulling himself back in. Penny nodded and looked over his shoulder at Sergeant Beal who smiled back nervously. For the first time ever, Edwards was going to put three jumpers out in quick succession over the drop zone. Penny would be first, followed by Beal, and then Evans.

Penny felt the plane drop and then level out as the jump-side engine began to throttle back. Edwards motioned for him to move closer as the plane slowed to exit speed. For Penny, this was when he was most nervous, that first step and then the drop and howling wind wash, giving himself over to fate, and the twenty-four pounds of silk and nylon on his back and belly.

There were few things a person could do in life that reached the level of commitment that it took to step out of the open door of an airplane. Time, sound, and the perception of distance changed and distorted into fragmented images that replayed in the mind for hours, days, and even years after a jump. Penny barely heard Edwards shout "Go!" as he stepped out into the wind. He was beyond the control of any man, dropping, dropping, feeling the suspension lines ripping off his back, the cold exhaust-filled air rushing by his face and then the jolting pop of the canopy as it opened.

There was no greater adrenalin rush, no greater spark to the soul than sitting under an open canopy a thousand feet in the air.

Penny reached up, grabbed a handful of left riser, and pulled down, slowly turning the canopy. To his surprise, Sergeant Beal was floating forty yards away, also turning to the left.

"Yo, Sergeant Beal!" shouted Penny as loud as he could.

Beal twisted in the harness. "Eeeehaa!" he shouted back, the adrenalin putting a crack in his voice.

Penny looked to his right and spotted Evans' canopy as he was also turning into the wind, the large orange windsock at the far end of the drop zone clearly visible less than nine hundred feet below.

As Penny prepared to land, he held the canopy into the wind, slapping his feet and knees together, tucking his elbows in, and keeping his eyes on the horizon. Forty feet, thirty, twenty, and then down with a grunt into the tall grass, the canopy settling to the ground like some large white jellyfish.

Seconds later Beal and Evans dropped into the grass, executing nearly perfect PLFs. If there had been a reporter nearby or someone who had taken a photograph of the three men as they walked away laughing and joking about the jump, they would have captured something monumental in the annals of American military history. They would have seen the birth of an operational idea shepherded by men with vision and an unusual level of courage. It was the execution of an idea that would change the methods of war. They would have seen the birth of American Airborne.

For the next week and a half, the jumping continued with each man in the unit getting in five jumps, a number that would be standard for future Paratrooper training. At the end of two weeks with little fanfare besides a graduation dinner courtesy of the United States Army, the gear was packed, the trucks were loaded, and the fifty men that came to an obscure airstrip in southern New Jersey loaded the aircraft that had brought them and flew away.

Two hours into the flight on their way back to Camp Claiborne, Edwards climbed over and around the boxes and gear that had been secured in the Center of the DC-3. He was looking for Penny who was sleeping in one of the web seats near the back of the plane. Finally getting to an open spot, he sat down, nudging Penny to wake up. "Hey, I got something I need to give you," he announced reaching into a canvas kit bag.

Penny sat up yawning. "What's going on?" he asked shivering from the cold. Edwards pulled a thick manila envelope out of the bag and tossed it on his lap.

"Payday!" he announced with a smile.

Penny picked up the fat bundle. "Payday?"

Edwards nodded, "Yep, the pay master from Fort Dix delivered it yesterday. Go on, take a look. I think you'll be happy."

Still not sure what was going on, he opened the envelope and was stunned to see a thick wad of new hundred dollar bills wrapped tightly in rubber bands inside. He looked at Edwards, shocked by the size of the bundle. "How much is in here?"

Edwards smiled, "Seven thousand five hundred dollars. It's our pay for helping the Army set up the program."

"Are we splitting this?" asked Penny, overwhelmed to be holding this amount of money.

Edwards laughed. "Nope, that's yours." He reached in the bag and pulled out another thick bundle. "See, I got one too. Just like we agreed. What do you think?"

Penny thought for a moment while looking at the money smiling. "If I had known the Army pays this well, I would have worked with them a lot sooner."

Edwards laughed and stood up, holding on to the static line cable. "You earned it, Penny. Now, I'm going to get one of those box lunches. I'll let you get back to sleep."

Penny nodded and watched as Edwards started climbing back over the cargo and sleeping soldiers on his way to the front of the plane. As he looked at the bundle of cash, his mind was a blur. *Seven thousand dollars could buy a house*, he thought, *or a car, maybe two cars. Jesus, this was a lot of money.* Looking around at the other men who appeared to be sleeping soundly close by, he stuffed the money back in the envelope and carefully put it under the heavy coat he had been using as a pillow.

There was no way he would be able to sleep now he thought laying back down. Hell, as excited as he was he might never sleep again.

Chapter Twenty-Four

It was early November and the snow had begun to fall ending what had been a horrendous fire season in the Bitterroots. Thousands of acres had burned, and the death toll had now risen to four. The last fire of the season had started up on the Idaho-Montana border near Lost Trail Pass. A lightning strike had hit a cabin at four in the morning setting it ablaze and killing the young family of three sleeping inside. Penny had responded to the call along with the rest of the crew and was there at dawn when the bodies had been pulled out of what remained of the structure.

The parents looked to be in their early thirties though it was hard to tell due to the deep charring of the skin. What had hit Penny the hardest was watching as they wrapped the body of the little girl in a sheet before carrying her out to the waiting Missoula ambulance. Someone in the group of men there that cold morning had said she was probably nine or ten and had been found under her parent's bed, still clutching a small plastic doll. It had melted in her hands.

The family had been known to the community. The husband, a carpenter, had been picking up odd jobs around the Darby area. The mother and her daughter had been picking and canning berries to sell to the locals.

Penny sat on the back of the station's pickup and watched as the ambulance drove away carrying the bodies of the family. Edwards walked up and tossed a shovel into the bed of the truck. "You ready to go? Nothing else we can do here." His face was covered in black soot from digging in the burned debris.

"Why do you think God allowed that?" questioned Penny tossing his own shovel and axe into the bed of the pickup. He walked around to the passenger side door and slid onto the bench seat. "I mean, what did they do to deserve to die like that? Jesus, Mitch, she was just a little kid."

Edwards slid in behind the wheel and started the truck. "Shit, I don't know, Penny. If I stopped and thought about all the bad things that happen to good people, I think I'd drown myself in the Salmon. You gonna be okay?"

Penny lit a cigarette and sat back thinking as the first rays of an early fall sunrise sprayed a brilliant gold and pink over the Saw Tooth's to the east. "Yeah, I'm okay. It's just at times like this, Mitch, I wonder if God is really paying attention."

Edwards pulled onto the gravel road leading back to the station, trying hard to think of something to say. He could tell that Penny was deeply upset by what he had seen and was trying to get his mind around some kind of reasonable answer. Coming up empty, he kept quiet, letting the wheel noise rolling on fresh gravel fill the void. He had no idea why that family had to die that way. Bad luck, fate, some twisted cosmic logic…who the hell knew? It was just life, a hard death no one deserved. Some things are just too terrible to think about and, goddamn, this was one of them.

**

Later that day, Penny and the other members of his class were repacking the new A7 parachutes given to them by the Army for their help in New Jersey. Edwards walked toward the men with final instructions for the season. He had just returned from Pearson's office where he had learned that the CCC camp would not be opening up in the spring. Evidently things were getting better job-wise in the rest of country, and the program was to be scaled back. He wasn't sure how he felt about the sudden drawdown of potential firefighters, a group of folks he had used extensively for two very heavy fire seasons.

"Hey, guys, listen up," he said stepping into the shed. "I have some news." He set a small cardboard box on the packing table. "I just came back from Pearson's office. The word has come down from DC that the Smoke Jump program has been thoroughly funded and will become an operational part of the US Forest Service as of December first."

"What does that mean?" asked Penny, pinning the last flap closed on the parachute container he was packing.

Edwards smiled. "It means, guys, that we are now an official Forest Service Program and will be treated as such. We won't be looked at as just some crazy folks who jump out of airplanes. Congratulations, fellas, you represent class one. You're officially designated as *"Smoke Jumpers"* by the United States Government."

Outside, the dull drone of the DC-3 from Missoula could be heard coming in on final approach. "Oh, and I just got a little gift from the Army that I thought you might like." He picked up the box. "Here's the deal. The Army, with a little help from us, is going to develop and train Paratroopers for military operations. One of their Generals designed a graduation pin that will be given to the guys who pass the training. He sent me a box of the first pins made. They call them *Jump Wings*. He said you guys can have some of the first ones made. Here you go. Wear them proudly, gents."

Penny took one of the small silver pins from the box. It was a small metal parachute with curled wings on each side. The pin was no longer than an inch. "You think these will catch on?" he asked, clipping the pin on front of his shirt pocket.

Edwards laughed. "Well, at least you have a souvenir for all your efforts if they don't."

The DC-3 roared up near the shed, throttling back both engines filling the air with the now familiar smell of engine exhaust. "Okay, guys, this is the last flight out of Missoula till spring." announced Edwards shouting above the engine noise. "I need all you guys back here in April. We will be starting a new class. Penny, did you say you would be staying in Darby over the winter?"

"Yeah, rented the Simpson's house over on the west side of town. Hell, half these guys are staying with me."

Edwards laughed. "Good, make sure they pay part of the rent. Okay, guys, again - congratulations. I know this is all kind of informal, considering all the work that went into getting the program up and running, but 1941 is going to be our year. Like I said, you're all on the pay-role now as permanent party so I need you back in April. Everybody understand?"

Penny nodded. "You got it, boss. We will pack up here and start shutting everything down."

Edwards thought for a moment as he looked at the young faces of the men he had trained over the last two months. He could not have asked for a more dedicated group of people to work with. "Okay, fellas, been a pleasure. I'm heading back out to California for the winter. I'll see you all next spring." He shook hands with each one and then quickly left the shed, not wanting to get sappy with emotion.

With an odd melancholy, Penny watched as Edwards trotted out to the waiting plane. He had been charged with closing down the station for the winter, securing the new gear and making sure the buildings and grounds were locked up. Ending his second year on the mountain, he could not have been happier. He was proud of the fact that Edwards and Pearson trusted him with so much responsibility, a real honor for someone so young.

Even though he was still deeply bothered by the house fire that had killed the young family earlier that morning, he had begun to accept the fact that there was nothing he could have done to prevent it. God, fate, or just terrible luck had killed them and, no matter how he felt about it, that kind of awful ending would have been the same. Mitch was right, he thought, stacking the last of the packed parachutes into the back of the pickup. He simply could not allow the image of that dead little girl to become something he dwelled on. She was gone and that was that. The sooner he put the incident behind him the better.

As he slid in behind the wheel of the pickup, he thought about his father and what his reaction might have been to the life he had now. Driving along the dirt track that led up to the main gravel road, he played out the same scene he had run a thousand times before in his mind, the one where he drove the Forest Service truck into the yard of his home in Kansas. His parents were sitting on the porch, healthy and whole. The sun was out. The dust was gone. He spent the entire day in the warm sunshine telling them about his adventures. Heaven should be so good.

***

Edwards sat in the web seat by the closed cargo door. He leaned back, going over in his mind the things he had left unsaid to Penny and the rest of the class. Over the last several months, they had trusted him with their lives and had helped birth a program that he was convinced had merit. They had proven him right and, in doing so, had given him a solid legacy, something few men achieve in a lifetime of effort. As he felt the plane climb through the clear Montana sky, he regretted leaving them as quickly as he did.

Edwards remembered something his father had told him the week before he died of a massive heart attack while tending his garden. He had been visiting his parents in Naperville, Illinois, on a hot July afternoon after one of his European trips. His father had wanted him to see how tall his tomato plants had grown. He had never seen the old man happier as he moved through the knee-high vines laden with tomatoes talking nonstop about the spray he was using to keep the worms away, about how much water he was using just before sundown. It was like he had to say as much as possible before he would not be able to speak at all, as if the gift of conversation was going to be taken away. Edwards had been genuinely surprised by his father's animation on that hot afternoon, his demeanor normally one of quiet, deep reservation.

He remembered when his father seemed to catch himself rambling on. He had stood there in his shirt sleeves and tattered brown fedora looking up into the sun as if he were listening to music only he could hear. "You know, Mitch, never pass up an opportunity to tell the people you care about how you feel about them. You may not get another chance."

He remembered that the comment had caught him off guard; it was not something his father would normally say. He could count on one hand the number of times they had had a conversation of any depth. Maybe the old man had been saying good-bye in the only way he knew, trying to leave him one last bit of wisdom before that final ride. If that had been his intention, his timing had been uncanny; he died just three days later. They found his body face down in the dirt he had raked, hoed, and planted for years. His mother never planted a garden again.

He checked his watch. In twelve hours he would be hopping another flight out of Missoula to Reno. If things stayed on schedule, he should be with his woman late tomorrow night. Sitting back in his seat, watching the dark green Montana landscape drift by far below, he decided to treat himself when they landed. He would head over to the Stockman's bar downtown, order a medium-rare Porterhouse with all the trimmings, and wash it all down with the best draft beer in Montana. Yeah, on days like this a decent meal and a couple of cold beers balanced one's perspective of the world. He had been riding a pretty good streak lately, accomplishing everything he had hoped for, and he wondered just how long it was all going to last. How long would the world he had created for himself hold together? He knew in his gut that the dark problems taking place on the other side of the ocean were closing and fast. Things were about to change. A cosmic shift was in the works, and everyone was going to be affected.

In the past, whenever physical or emotional conflict was close, he would run, wrapping himself in the livable rationalization that it was better to be an observer, someone detached from personal, blood-colored drama. He had become a professional spectator, someone with no real skin in the game.

Little did he know just how much skin, blood, and bone would be required in this next phase of his life. It would be a deadly contest he would be unable to run from. If he only knew.

Chapter Twenty-Five

Hans' unit was only supposed be in the village of Mien for a week, two weeks at most. In reality two months had passed since their arrival, a delay in movement ordered directly from Berlin. After two weeks of almost non-stop patrolling in and around the town and not seeing any more French resistance, the patrols had been cut back dramatically. Now, if a squad ventured out past the main crossroads a mile from the village once during the week, it was rare. Most of the time the platoon carried on as if in garrison back in Bad Tolz as opposed to holding a line outside the wire. Tanks manned the check points so there was little for the infantry to do, a condition that increased Hans' agitation by the day. He did not sign up for the SS to sit in some French back-water village getting fat. He would have loved to have someone to shoot.

For all the pre-invasion talk of the French resistance fighting to the death, it simply hadn't happened. There had been fairly intense fighting against the French Army at the Maginot line for several weeks, but in the open countryside, there had been no resistance.

Over the last month village life had returned to near normal levels, the villagers doing whatever they could to maintain peace between the platoon of SS and the town's citizens. Some of the men in Hans' unit were even seeing a few of the local women, something Hans had no feelings about one way or another. If his men wanted to spend their off time with French whores, what did he care.

For him, it was just one more reason to hate the French. He despised them for their weakness; hated them for the way they skulked around like beaten dogs whenever he walked the street. To his way of thinking, the French deserved to be conquered. Anyone not fighting for their country or women till the last breath did not deserve to live.

For the last week Volkmann had been back and forth from the Division headquarters a lot more than usual. He would leave early and get back after dark having a late supper with the officers from the Panzer unit parked just west of the town every evening. Hans received any information he needed the following morning from Lieutenant Steiner of the Tenth Panzer Corp. Assigned to Hans' platoon, the twenty-eight year-old second year officer looked to be about twelve.

His erudite upbringing and high level of education were evident in his speech and the manner in which he conducted himself. He was from Dresden, the only son of a successful financer, a loyal and influential member of the Nazi party, and he moved with confidence in the company of other officers.

In Hans' mind the kid was a dilettante, someone with family connections that had given him the opportunities and privileges in life that he hadn't had. He hadn't been interested enough to find out if the fresh faced Lieutenant had seen any action prior to showing up in France, not that it would have changed his opinion about the little shit. As far as he was concerned, if you had not been part of the Polish campaign, then you had not been in real combat. From what little he had picked up about him, he hadn't been a part of the Tenth Panzer when they rolled into Poland. That alone was enough to dislike him.

Hans had been up for an hour now. He carefully disassembled the P40 machinegun and laid the pieces on the table while his coffee simmered on the small coal stove in the corner of the room. Mueller was lying on the cot on the other side of the room rereading the letter he had received from his girlfriend almost two weeks ago. There had been no letters since.

"I think she is cheating on me," announced Mueller holding the letter up to his nose sniffing. "There's no perfume on this one. She always puts perfume on her letters."

Hans slid the bolt carrier back into the MP40 receiver. "Maybe she forgot. Women forget shit all the time."

Mueller swung his feet around and sat up on the edge of the cot. "What do you know about women? You're not married. You don't even have a girlfriend."

Hans snapped the upper and lower machinegun pieces together. "I know all about women," he replied shaking his head. "I was raised with my sister. She had her head up her ass most of the time. They're all like that."

Mueller snorted a laugh and laid back down, sniffing the letter again. "I know the bitch is cheating," he mumbled. "I just know it."

Hans pushed a loaded magazine into his weapon. "So what do you expect her to do? She probably had her feet in the air an hour after we left town. Jesus, who needs her?"

"You're a cynical bastard," replied Mueller carefully folding the letter and putting it in his shirt pocket. "No wonder you don't have a woman in your life."

Before Hans could reply, Lieutenant Steiner walked into the room. Another thing that annoyed Hans about the young officer was that his uniform always looked like he had just stepped off a parade field; it was immaculate. He was a tanker for Christ's sake and tanks are filthy - covered in oil, mud, and grease. How could anyone who rode around in those things be so goddamned clean? It was unnatural.

"Sergeant, just wanted to let you know we are leaving the area in one hour," announced Steiner pulling up a chair by the fire. "You need to let the rest of your platoon know."

"Leaving?"

Stiener smiled. "That's right, Sergeant. Looks like we are headed east. Could be seeing some action soon." He rubbed his hands together like an excited child. "Get us back in the war."

Hans sat back in his chair. "Have you seen much action yet, Sir?" He meant to sound polite but the question came out harsh.

Mueller, now pulling on his boots, looked over at Hans with an expression that said. "Shut the hell up, you idiot."

"Well, since you asked, Sergeant, we were at the Maginot. I lost three of my tanks and nine of my men fighting the French. Why do you ask?"

Hans thought for a moment, instinctively knowing that he needed to be very careful with his response. The young officer was now locking in a hard gaze. "Just curious," replied Hans smiling, surprised at how well the young officer stood his emotional ground. Maybe there was more to this pup than he realized.

"Anyway," announced Steiner slapping his thighs and standing up, "you need to get the rest of your platoon ready to move. The trucks will be here within the hour."

"Yes, Sir." nodded Hans.

Steiner straightened his tunic while looking at Hans. "I know you by reputation, Sergeant. You don't have to worry about me doing my job in contact with the enemy."

Hans smiled. "I meant no offense, Sir."

Steiner thought for a moment. "Of course you did. People have underestimated me before because of the way I look. You should not make that same mistake."

"No, Sir."

Steiner nodded. "Gentleman." He turned and walked out of the room.

Mueller pulled on his tunic, shaking his head. "You know, that guy is not someone you want to irritate. I don't think he cares much for the SS and you're not helping. Christ, he has connections."

Hans picked up his weapon. "You know it's really good that we are leaving this crap hole. You're sounding more and more like one of these village midwives." He walked out of the room while slinging the machinegun.

"Asshole," mumbled Mueller following him out.

Steiner had been correct about the quick departure. An hour later, Hans along with the rest of his unit were making their way north by truck. Rain had ushered them into the village two months earlier and now following them out. Hans watched as Mueller tried to light a cigarette in the driving rain. "You would think the bastards could have put the canvas on top!" shouted Mueller ripping the soggy cigarette out of his mouth in frustration. "Goddamn it!"

Hans laughed as the rain dripped off the rim of his helmet. "It's a glorious day, my friend," he replied looking up into the grey sky. "The rain is washing away our sins. We are getting back in the war where we belong."

Mueller pulled the collar of his rain poncho tight around his neck. "I belong by the fire; I don't like to be wet *and* cold!" He shouted at the driver who couldn't hear him above the truck noise. "How fucking hard would it be to put the canvas on?"

Hans smiled at the corporal's agitation and pointed to the floor between Mueller's feet. "The gods of war have heard you!" he shouted just as a low peel of thunder rolled across the French countryside.

Mueller looked under his seat. "Son-of-a-bitch," he said dragging out the large bundled canvas top. "Why didn't you say something earlier? Jesus Christ?"

Hans sat back and watched as the men quickly unrolled the large canvas and draped it over the hoops overhead, plunging the truck bed into a wet darkness. After a moment, he lit a dry cigarette and by the orange glow of the match handed it to Mueller. "You see, my cold, wet friend, all things work out for the righteous."

Mueller took the smoke, still mad at getting soaked. "You're a goddamned sadist," he announced after taking a long drag, the air now heavy with the smell of strong French tobacco. "You're crazy!"

Hans smiled in the dark as the rain continued to pound down on the canvas roof. Yes, isn't it wonderful, he thought. He could not have been happier, gods of war indeed - loved the way that sounded.

Chapter Twenty-Six

As the winter of '41 settled in, Penny found a genuine peace of spirit he had never felt before. Three of his smoke jumping teammates moved into the big rental house giving the environment the feel of family. Penny picked up a bartending job for the winter in Hamilton, a town twenty miles away from Darby. The job consisted of filling mugs of draft beer from the taps and running plates of food from the back grill to the bar. It didn't pay much, but the food was free and the atmosphere friendly. The other roommates took jobs in restaurants and cafes that serviced the year-round logging and ranching clientele in and around the Missoula-Hamilton area.

After turning eighteen in late January, Penny became even more aware of the growing sounds of war reverberating throughout the country. The newspapers were full of stories of Germany's non-stop aggression and the fall of country after country under the Nazis' advance. Poland, Holland, and now France had all surrendered to the Hitler Regime. For Penny and the rest of the guys on his team, it wasn't so much "if" they joined the military but "when".

Even in the outlands of rural Montana in early 1941, the growing threat and unease of war could be felt by every logger, rancher, and hard-rock miner living there. Over the course of the winter Penny had received several letters from Captain Barns talking about how well the new Army parachute units were doing and thanking him again for his help with the program. In his last letter he mentioned that, if Penny ever decided to go into the military, he should let him know. He said the new Airborne unit could use an experienced man like him. It was something Penny was now thinking about more and more as the days went by. He had been impressed with the paratroopers he had worked with in New Jersey. They wore self-confidence like a badge. The general comradery of the team, the feeling of being a part of something bigger than himself, appealed to him.

By late February, early March, the heavy snow that had buried the high line peaks of the Saw Tooth Mountains had begun to subside. Down below, large patches of sweet grass and new bud wild flowers started to appear in the meadows and windward hillsides, drawing large numbers of deer and elk for the spring feed. They dotted the landscape for miles like grazing cattle.

By the end of March, Penny was finally able to drive Edward's old truck through what little snow still blocked the Sealy Lake road leading to the Ranger Station. He was anxious to open up the buildings and check on the gear that had been left for the winter. His biggest concern was the condition of the station roof, wondering if the weight of the heavy snowfall that year had collapsed the building, not an uncommon occurrence in the area. To his relief, Penny found the station intact, having survived the long winter without damage from the snow.

In Edwards' latest letter he mentioned that he would be arriving in Missoula the first week of April. By April fifteenth he wanted the Smoke Jumpers on station ready to go wherever they were needed. It would be their first season as full time official Smoke Jumpers employed by the US Forest Service.

Penny had informed Mrs. Simpson down in Darby that he would not be renting the house now that the station was being opened. She had graciously accepted his last month payment letting him know that the place would be available next fall if he needed it. For reasons she kept to herself, she had no plans to rent to anyone else.

For Penny, the small routine things in his life now were the most important. He had friends, people who cared about him. Most of all, he had value as a person. People were depending on him, a responsibility he was grateful for and did not take for granted. Montana was now home; its open sky and incredible natural beauty had seeded itself deep in his heart. A connection sealed by blood and fire, Montana had marked his soul.

It took him and the rest of the fifteen-man crew a full week after arriving to get the station opened up, the bull dozers running, and all the smoke jumping gear unpacked and inspected. It was a glorious Montana spring that year, the multi-colored wild flowers thick in the meadows and the dark green sweet grass seeming to grow an inch by the day. Even though the news from Europe had been increasingly grim, the mood at Sealy was filled with optimism and excitement about the new program.

Penny was anxious to get back into the woods, back to the high line wildness of bear and elk, where the days were short and the star-lit nights held a special blue magic that could not be explained to anyone who had not seen it. In the past two years he had stood on rocky ridgelines while the whole earth below seemed to be on fire and, in those moments, those brief slivers of time, he bathed in an intoxicating peace. He felt no joy at seeing the woods burn but understood in an instant his small part in the drama of the moment, a feeling of clarity about who he was, what he was supposed to do, of who he was supposed to be. He was a fire fighter and would always be drawn to the oddly familiar, heart touching smell of wood smoke.

As he pulled one of the packed canopies from the deployment bag in the packing shed, he remembered some of the good times back in Kansas - hopeful times before the dust closed in on the country like a shroud. The old men had said that the dust would pass, that the rains would come, that nothing this bad or tough could remain too long. God simply would not allow it.

The prayers of the faithful had gone up every Sunday from the Baptists, the Methodists, and even the stoic Lutherans all across Kansas. The prayers were sent up through sunbaked roofs, over the dusty brown fields, and across the drying creek beds with a plea to God for rains, fervent prayers for a divine rescue that never came. He remembered sitting on the front porch with his parents many times when it was too hot to be in the house and watching the heat lighting flash on the dark horizon, desperately wanting to smell that sweet summer rain and to hear thunder.

It was well after one in the afternoon in the second week, when they heard the familiar drone of a DC-3 making its way through Lost Trail Pass still miles away. Penny stepped off the porch of the station and raised his binoculars to watch the plane on final approach. He never tired of seeing the planes land and take off, fascinated by the idea that something that big could fly. As he watched the silver Douglas slowly descending through the clear Montana sky, he thought about how good it would be to see his friend and mentor Edwards, the man who had given him so much over the last two years.

After working in and around the different aircraft over the last year, Penny could now recognize the different sounds the engine made taking off and landing at the station - the throttle backs, the fuel cuts, the prop feathering, and the countless other sounds the planes made as they came and went. Now, as he watched the DC-3, he heard a strange high pitch whine coming over the top of the normal engine noise. To Penny it sounded like some large part of one of the Pratt Whitney engines was moving way too fast, like it was about to spin itself to pieces. And then it happened. In an instant, as he was thinking of it, he watched in horror through his binoculars as the left engine on the descending plane suddenly exploded in a brilliant orange and red fire ball as if hit by a missile. The left wing instantly dropped nearly ninety degrees, sending the plane into a steep dive.

Penny and the rest of the crew were already running full out towards the end of the strip as the Douglas desperately attempted to level off once more before spinning into the ground at over a hundred miles an hour. Even from nearly two football fields away, Penny could feel the sickening vibration through the ground of the plane's impact as he ran towards the crash. The woods and what was left of the heavily loaded plane were now on fire as Penny made his way through the broken and burning wreckage. "Edwards!" he shouted spotting a crumbled body lying in the tall grass. As he grew close, he could see that the man had been nearly torn in half from the impact. Rolling him onto his back he recognized one of the young pilots from Missoula, a copilot named Craig. Desperate to find survivors, he carefully walked around the shattered remains of the plane, shielding his face from the intense heat of the flames.

It would take another two hours for the blaze to finally die down, the grass fire around the crash to be put out, and before they could find the rest of the crew. It would take another full week of checking dental records by the Medical Examiner in Missoula before the burned remains of Mitch Edwards and the other three crewmen were finally identified. In the weeks following the fatal crash, the results of the investigation revealed that a severed fuel-line, possibly due to a bird strike, had been the cause. For Penny, finding the cause of the crash was of little comfort. He had lost another person he cared for, someone who had given him the benefit of the doubt in all things and provided opportunities he could never have imagined. It was a crushing loss personally and to the Smoke Jumper program as a whole. For Penny there would always be a small painful wound just above his heart, a wound caused by the death of his friend - Mitch Edwards.

There was talk of suspending the program indefinitely, a point of view quickly corrected by people like Pearson and many others within the department who held the vision and the support for the Smoke Jumper program. Men stepped forward and demanded that the legacy of Mitch Edwards not end in the firey plane crash in the outlands of Montana. Too much effort had gone into the endeavor. Too much blood had been sacrificed for it not to continue.

Chapter Twenty-Seven

Hans was less than impressed with the enemy; for days now they had slaughtered them by the hundreds. Having kicked off Operation Barbarosa, a massive offensive onto Russian soil, a week earlier, his unit was now at the most forward spear of advance. Some of the Russian troops hadn't even had rifles or any weapons for that matter. During the height of battle, the unarmed waved huge red flags adorned with the bright yellow hammer and sickle of the Red Army. In Hans' mind, it had been a pathetic bravado in the face of certain death, a waste of time and life. No wonder the Russians were losing the war.

Now within four hundred kilometers of Moscow, they still faced only moderate resistance. Conflict on the Eastern Front had turned into a one-sided route. For Hans, it was inconceivable that the Reds could keep losing this many people and continue to fight for much longer. At this rate it should all be over by fall.

He and the rest of his platoon slowly walked through the latest tangle of over a hundred dead and dying Red Army soldiers hit by German artillery earlier in the morning. They had been the last dug-in defense on the outskirts of Smolensk, a once thriving Russian city of fifty thousand residents. The German barrage of the town had started just before four in the morning and had ended just after ten, smashing to pieces the last remnants of the Soviet 12th and 13th Corp. Hans' unit had been sent in as a reconnaissance probe to assess the effect of the barrage that had pounded the city for hours. Now, all that could be heard was the pop and snap of smoldering fires as a heavy acrid black smoke from burning Soviet equipment drifted across the field. Their guns, fortifications, and equipment had been no match for the ferocious German artillery.

Hans rolled up his sleeves and lit a cigarette. It was only ten-thirty in the morning but the air was already thick with humidly, the temperature well into the eighties. He stood and surveyed the twisted and torn bodies around him while taking in a deep lungful of smoke. It was amazing what heavy artillery did to the human body. Many of the dead that lay nearby had no visible wounds, their eyes open in vacant stares, hearts and lungs turned to pulp, killed instantly by the massive over-pressure of exploding shells.

He knelt down to study the glassy stare of a soldier that could not be more than seventeen years old. Even in death, his uniform looked two sizes too big, the buttoned collar looking as if it would circle a neck twice his size. Shrapnel had blown off the entire lower left side of his face and jaw, opening a massive wound all the way to an exposed spinal column in the neck. Hans stood up and stuck the toe of his boot into the kid's wound, slowly pushing down until he heard and felt the neck bones snap under the pressure.

Mueller walked up sweating from the early morning heat, a limp cigarette dangling from his lips. "They're all dead," he announced pushing his helmet to the back of his head. "The shelling killed all of them." He let his M40 machinegun hang low on the sling.

"You sound disappointed," replied Hans shaking the gore off the toe of his boot.

"No disappointment here. As far as I'm concerned, if the Luftwaffe and artillery kill every one of these bastards and I finish the war without firing a shot, I am happy." He took his helmet off and quickly rubbed his head. "How far do we go into town?" he asked, still scratching his itching scalp.

Hans brought the binoculars up to his eyes as a cloud of black smoke drifted by. "There's a large building, ah, I'd say about three hundred meters due east. Looks like some kind of grain silo." He handed the binoculars to Mueller. "Take a look. I think we should head over there. Might be a good place for an OP."

Mueller was quiet while looking through the glass. "That's pretty far into town," he announced shaking his head. "What if we run into a bigger unit of Reds than this? Not sure we can fight our way out of there if we run into something with numbers." He handed the binoculars back. "But that's your call."

Hans thought for a moment and then flicked his cigarette butt into the dead Russian's face. "Okay, pass the word to the rest of the platoon - we are headed to the silo."

For Hans, the decision to move in a direction was not so much a geographic consideration but one based on opportunity of finding and killing the enemy. He could care less how many of "them" were at any given location. He firmly believed that he simply could not be killed by an inferior soldier, an inferior human being for that matter. Over the last year he had been in many situations where he had been out-numbered and, in some cases out-gunned by hostile forces, yet he had prevailed every time, walking away without a scratch over and over again. Having that kind of luck in battle after battle could not be attributed to blind chance. It had to be something more, something spiritual, something that wielded great power. Walking through the bloody ruins of the shattered Soviet 13th Corp, he smiled, relishing the near sexual ecstasy of moving through a smoldering battlefield littered with dead enemies. The smell, the sounds, and the images of total carnage burned deep into his brain - images terribly wonderful.

He heard the faint cry of a wounded soviet soldier begging for water behind him and then the familiar muffled pistol shot. The SS had a standing order from Himmler himself not to take prisoners, an order that was being followed to the letter. By the time the platoon reached the open meadow just below the silo, Hans had lost track of the number of pistol shots fired. Orders were orders.

It took over an hour to reach the base of the silo that was now little more than a bombed out shell. The artillery barrage had blasted away most of the roof and left the surrounding building pocked-marked from heavy shrapnel hits. The only signs of life were two scrawny chickens that walked out of the ruined silo as Hans walked in. "It's clear," he announced stepping back out into the sun.

The rest of the platoon began setting up a defensive perimeter as Mueller walked up pulling his map out of his tunic pocket. With a grunt, he sat down next to Hans putting his back against the silo wall. "Looks like everyone ran off," he announced unfolding the map. "According to this, we've gone three, ah, maybe four hundred meters past the point where we should have stopped." He looked over smiling, sweat and grime running down the side of his face. "If I did not know better, I would say you're trying to get me killed."

Hans laughed as he took off his helmet. "Been trying since Poland, my friend," he replied, rubbing his sweat-matted hair. "The problem is that your luck is too strong." He took the last of his Pervitin methamphetamine tablets, from his shirt pocket. "Here, I have two left. Take one," he said dropping a tablet into Mueller's hand. "That should get us through the day."

Mueller quickly popped the pill into his mouth and chewed it, grimacing from the bitter taste. He along with the rest of the platoon had been up for three days now without sleep, having moved nearly a kilometer with little effort deep into enemy lines - the magic benefit of the pills in the gold foil wrapper.

Within minutes of swallowing the meth, Hans felt the now familiar sensations of the Pervitin coursing through his body - the strange heat in the palms of his hands, the rushing sound in his ears, the slight cramping in his gut, followed by a huge rush of energy and alertness that could not be duplicated without the pills. It gave him an emotionally detached state of mind, a feeling that his body was moving and reacting on its own, a sensation of working at top speed all while he hovered high above like some passive winged observer, an observer totally unaffected by what was happening below.

As the rest of the platoon sat in the sun, Hans watched as others in his line of sight took their Pervitin. The unit now seemed to be feeding off the stuff, he thought, taking a long drink of warm water from his canteen. A sudden bolt of panic shot through his body as a spider, black as coal and as big as his hand, suddenly appeared out of the corner of his eye crawling near his leg. He spun to his feet in a flurry of dust and dirt, startling Mueller who jumped up, weapon at the ready. "Jesus!" he shouted. "What? What is it?"

Hans, feeling as if his heart would pound a hole through his chest, stared at the ground where he saw the massive spider. "It was a spider...this big!" he replied wide-eyed, bringing his hands together, still searching the ground. "I swear. It was the biggest spider I have ever seen."

Mueller, now more amused than scared, chuckled as he picked up his helmet. "It's the Pervitin. Makes you see shit that isn't there. You see spiders - I see fucking snakes." He picked up his weapon and map smiling. "Can we go now?"

Still not convinced it was a hallucination, Hans kicked his helmet just in case the spider was hiding underneath. Mueller laughed while walking over to a pile of rubble to take a piss. "No spiders, my friend!" he shouted over his shoulder. "It's all in your head!"

Hans picked up his helmet and weapon, trying to shake the image of the huge bug from his mind. He had been afraid of spiders since childhood, and now seeing something that big right out of his nightmares, imagined or not, was terrifying. If this was truly a side effect of the pills he was taking, he thought motioning for the platoon to start moving, then maybe he would stop taking so much of the stuff. "Jesus," he whispered slinging his weapon. From now on, he would give his ration of pills to someone else; he could do without any more bad magic. Little did he know, the bad magic had no intention of letting him go. The darkness in the hearts of men at war was justgetting started. There were even bigger spiders waiting in the dark.

Chapter Twenty-Eight

For Penny, the death of Edwards was a deep down blow to the soul that took weeks to fully feel. The station just wasn't the same without him and everyone associated with the Smoke Jumper Program felt it. Pearson had placed a call to Washington days after the crash informing that a new operations officer for the Smoke Jumper Organization would be needed. But a month had gone by and still no one had been appointed. It would be tough to find anyone with the zeal and dedication for smoke jumping that Mitch Edwards had carried. Maybe impossible.

Fortunately, there had only been two small fires so far: one up on Lost Trail Pass by the newly paved highway and one large grass fire a mile outside of Darby. Penny had taken the lead on both, knocking them down with just a small crew in hours.

In addition to the lack of leadership for the program, a new plane had not yet arrived at the station or had even been allotted thus far, a fact that Penny found deeply troubling. Maybe the powers at be really did not want to continue the program and the death of Edwards was an excuse to not put anything else into it. It was all speculation on his part of course, but with the lack of any real news about the program, rumors and fears burned hot.

Pearson had made it clear that he wanted Penny to run the station, maintain the radios, keep the vehicles running, and carry the responsibility for the general clean-up of the grounds. Because the Civilian Conservation Corps was winding down, Penny saw a lot more of Pearson than in the past when their paths had rarely crossed. They now spent several evenings a week sitting on the station's porch drinking beer and watching the star-filled Montana sky. Conversations after supper were like those of most men who guarded their emotions, running the gamut from politics to women, conversations that would eventually get back around to how much both of them really missed their friend Mitch.

For weeks after the crash Penny would walk out to the cleared spot on the ground where the plane hit, trying to connect in some way with the man that had given him so much. He would sit on the mound of dirt where the landing gear had dug a two-foot trench in the hard packed dirt upon impact and try to remember all the things Mitch had taught him. As hard as he prayed and wished for answers, the only response had been the wind in the trees and the silent, clear blue sky over head. There could be no reason for the death of his friend as far as he was concerned. God or fate or whatever force that controlled the lives of men had checked out on this one, letting the precariousness of life have its way. In a flash, four good and decent men had died, incinerated in the wreckage of the plane they trusted.

For Penny, the pain and loss was enough to swear off organized religion all together; he wanted no part of it. Not getting any real answers from people who were supposed to know about this kind of thing had rubbed him raw emotionally, taking away what little faith he had left. The local pastor at the Lutheran church in Missoula had proclaimed at the service that it was "God's will," that some things the Almighty did could never be understood by mortal men.

In Penny's mind, if an all-knowing God dropped airplanes into the dirt at a hundred miles an hour killing four of his friends in the process, he did not see the need to follow Him. Shit, life was tough enough without the Maker of the universe trying to snuff out your candle whenever He liked. It was like having really bad odds in a rigged game as far as he was concerned. Mitch Edwards had been a good man and had deserved better than he had gotten.

***

It was late on a hot, dusty afternoon in mid-August. The mountain horse flies were thick, and the heavy scent of ponderosa pine hung heavy in the air when Penny heard a familiar sound that made his heart skip a beat. He was in the packing shed mending a riser on one of the harnesses when the low unmistakable drone of an approaching DC-3 could be heard in the distance. Excited, he trotted out of the shed in time to see the shiny Douglas drop down slowly below the treetops and then gently bounce onto the grassy strip a hundred yards away.

As the plane rolled closer, he quickly brushed away a tear. He had almost forgotten how beautiful the DC-3 really was. Seeing this one touch-down brought up waves of emotion, all of them good.

The pilot, a man that Penny had never seen before, slid the small side cockpit window open while feathering back the engines. "I'm looking for a guy named Reynolds!" he shouted over the engine as it wound down.

Penny stepped closer, mindful of the spinning prop. He pointed to himself. "That's me!" he shouted back.

The pilot smiled, gave him a thumbs up, and then slid the window closed. A minute later the plane's large side cargo door slid open and the man and several others that he had not seen before jumped down. The men were all dressed alike, wearing new khaki uniforms that resembled the military.

"Looks like you're the man I am supposed to see," announced the pilot stepping close as he extended a hand. Penny shook hands, not having a clue what was going on. "Pearson said you were young. Gosh, he wasn't kidding."

"You know Pearson?" asked Penny, ignoring the reference to his age.

"Sure do. He's the one that sent us up here." He turned to the men standing behind him. "Jack, go ahead and start unloading the gear." He took a thick folded envelope out of his back pocket and handed it to Penny. "Here's the official paper work for the aircraft and the crew which is all us. It's all in there. It's a whole bunch of government mumbo jumbo if you ask me. But then again, nobody's asking. Now, where do you want us to put our gear?"

Penny was still confused. "What are you talking about? Who are you guys? What's going on?"

The pilot smiled shaking his head. "So Pearson didn't give you a heads up about all this?"

"About all what?"

The young pilot laughed. "Geez, it's amazing the lack of communication going on around here. *We* are your new aircrew and aircraft - assigned to the US Department of Forestry Smoke Jumper Operation, which you are a big part of, as I am told. I'm Jim Collins, your new pilot. Now, where do we eat and sleep?"

***

Twenty-two hundred miles due west, a massive storm ripped past the rugged Oregon coast, lashing wind and rain gaining strength as it flew eastward into the Cascade Mountains. In two days it passed the Blue Mountain Range picking up speed as it blasted into the Rockies near the Idaho border. By the time it reached Montana, the storm had picked up huge amounts of cold air that mixed with the warmer coastal winds forming a static charge fueling spectacular lightning and heaven-shaking thunder. The lightning soon set a good portion of Western Montana on fire in spite of the rain. It would be the last major burn of the summer of '41, one that would test everything the hard men at Sealy Lake knew or thought they knew about fighting fires in the big timber.

In an ironic game of cosmic one-up-man-ship, a fire originating from the Far East would be set in the next five months, a conflagration of monstrous proportions inflaming the whole world, changing it forever. For Penny, the impact would be even greater on his life than the death of his friend Mitch.

No one on the planet would escape the flames this time - no one.

"It is forbidden to kill; therefore all murderers are punished unless they kill in large numbers and to the sound of trumpets."

Voltaire....

Chapter Twenty-Nine

"What's the point of fishing like that when you can just drop a twenty-four in the water and get as many fish as you want? I have one in my pack," announced Mueller lying back in the tall grass scratching his bare chest.

Hans flicked the line on the end of his makeshift pole into deeper water. They had been fishing from the bank of the Dnieper River and lounging in the sun for a good hour now. It was a welcome break from a week of bloody intense fighting with the retreating remnants of the 7th and 9th Russian Divisions. Their burned and bloated dead littered the ground for miles in all directions.

The rest of Hans' unit were either sleeping in the warm sun or sitting quietly beside the row of Tiger tanks along the road eating the first real meal they had had in days.

"You're missing the point," replied Hans squatting down. "Fishing is not totally about catching fish, my friend."

Thinking for a moment, Mueller took a long drag on his cigarette while squinting into the sun. "If it's not about getting fish, why the hell do it?"

"Didn't you ever fish when you were a kid?"

Mueller thought for a moment. "Nope, can't say I ever did; never cared for fish much."

"Then you missed out on something," replied Hans shaking his head. "It calms me down. Always has."

Mueller sat up, flicking his cigarette butt into the slow moving stream. "Never had the patience for it." He took a small half-full bottle of peach schnapps out of his pants' pocket, drained it in two swallows, and then tossed it into the water.

Hans looked over and smiled at his friend's appearance. The skin on his neck, face, and from the elbows down was tanned a deep brown from the sun. The rest of his shirtless body was strikingly pale, almost a light blue. He was still wearing his helmet, giving him the look of some filthy, half-starved vagrant who had found a bucket and put it on his head.

"Why are you still wearing your helmet?"

"Snipers," replied Mueller smiling, lying back in the grass. "You never know when one of those Red bastards is going to slither up and take a shot."

Hans laughed. "Jesus, Mueller, your skin is like a big white flag. With a target like that, I doubt anyone is going to shoot you in the head. Besides they're all dead."

Still laying on his back, Mueller closed one nostril with his index finger and blew the other clear. "I plan on surviving this shit. I have things to do after the war."

Hans chuckled. "What plans do you have? I think the Army suits you pretty well."

Mueller slowly sat up with a grunt and then stood up, letting his P40 machinegun hang loose on the sling. Constantly carrying the weapon over the last several months had worn the bluing off the side of the gun leaving a dull silver patina behind. The visual metaphor was not lost on Hans as he tossed his line out into the river. His whole unit was worn down, including himself - hammered flat both physically and emotionally in the non-stop push to Moscow.

Over the past two weeks they had moved so fast several times that they had outrun their supply convoy, leaving them dangerously low on ammunition and basic supplies, a mistake that could have cost them dearly if the Soviets had been able to mount any kind of sustained counter-attack. The Panzers were even slower, the constant equipment breakdowns often dropping movement to a crawl. At the current pace, Hans had serious doubts of reaching Moscow before Christmas even though they had been killing Reds wholesale since they crossed the border.

Mueller stepped closer to the edge of the bank opening his fly to piss. "What I plan to do first thing after the war is go find your sister," he said laughing.

Hans shook his head. "She will kill you in your sleep," he replied half serious. Besides, she likes men with lots of money. That's her style - a real bitch, a typical city girl."

Mueller shook off the last few drops and then buttoned his pants. "Not so, my friend. One night with me, and it will ruin her for any other man. She does not stand a chance. Women love me. It's a power they cannot refuse."

Hans sat down in the weeds, jamming the end of the pole into the soft dirt. He had heard Mueller talk about his alleged power over females since Poland but hadn't seen any evidence of his supposed ability yet. Even the older farm maid they came across just outside Smolensk last week had fought him the entire time they were searching her house for weapons. She definitely had not been soft butter in his hands.

The woman's screaming and lack of cooperation had become so annoying that Hans had walked back into the house after executing the three Soviet soldiers found hiding in a hay crib and shot her through the head. Her husband had sat in a chair by the door with his hands raised the entire time, not saying a word. Before pulling out of the area, Hans' unit had set every house in the village on fire, including hers. Even as the flames had consumed the house, the husband had not moved from the chair.

"Going to make an honest woman out of her," announced Mueller lighting another cigarette as he sat back down. "True love always wins." He handed the smoke to Hans who waved it off while lying back in the grass.

"There is no true love in this world," he said to the sky. "This is the closest thing to it. It's the best we can hope for."

Mueller looked out over the large slow moving river a moment and then back at Hans, shaking his head. "If I believed that," he replied picking up his pack and shirt, "I would shoot myself in the head." He walked off slowly heading for one of the mess trucks without saying another word.

As Hans drifted off to sleep the distant rumble of German artillery rolled in his ears. *True love*, he thought letting the crushing fatigue and then sleep have their way. *What a load of shit.*

***

A world away, where the realities of everyday life kept a steady rhythm through the seasons and the vagaries of nature, the first seventy-mile-long bolt of lightning split the predawn darkness like a massive jagged white dagger from heaven. The fifty-thousand degree bolt blasted through the tall Montana timber with enough force to char roots two feet under the wet soil. Within a span of ten minutes the entire west slope just south of the small nine building settlement of Sula, Montana, was on fire having been hit by no less than fifteen high-energy lightning strikes. It was several hours past sunrise before the first group of fire crews out of Missoula were even near the fire, a blaze that had already incinerated twenty acres an hour.

It would be another half hour before the Sealy Lake crew was notified that they were needed as fast as the DC-3 could fly. The Fire Boss on the ground had called in the Smoke Jumpers to run a cut line on the far side of the western slope to knock down as much potential fuel as possible.

For Penny and the rest of the nine-man crew the fear of what was to come was over-shadowed by a nearly giddy excitement at finally being able to do what they had trained for. As they walked single file to the running DC-3 in full gear, Penny felt the unmistakable presence of Mitch. As he climbed up the short ladder into the plane, he could almost hear his friend giving commands in that familiar easy tone that both directed and inspired.

Inside, Penny lifted the headset off the hook by the door. "Com check" he announced, adjusting the mic.

"We're good, Penny," replied the pilot. "Just got the coordinates from the Fire Boss. It's a tight DZ so I am going to have to make two passes. The ground crew will have red smoke on the leading edge. Are you good with that?"

"No sweat," replied Penny. "Just give me a two-minute countdown on the jump run."

"Roger that. Be advised, Penny, according to weather, the winds are seven out of the west, pushing ten. Everybody loaded up back there? We're rolling." Penny kicked the ladder away from the door as the plane slowly began its pre take-off roll to the far end of the field. As far as he was concerned, the jump was a "go" no matter how high the winds were. Too much had gone into the effort to get this unit up and functioning for it to be stopped now.

Thirty miles to the northeast, the Black Rock burn, as it was now called, ripped through the East Fork Junction settlement taking two houses, a large hay barn, and three horses secured in the stalls. Carl Stansman, a forty-five-year-old local rancher and owner of the property had barely escaped with his life when he made a futile attempt to free the horses. Several fire fighters who had arrived on the line minutes later saw Stansman stumbling out of the undergrowth half naked and deeply burned over most of his body. The intense heat had seared his lungs and throat cutting off his ability to speak which in turn made it impossible for him to tell the rescuers that his wife and aged mother were still back in one of the houses that by now was being consumed by the fast moving blaze. At the time no one could figure out why the burned rancher fought so hard as they tried to load him into the ambulance. With burns that severe, any sane man should have begged for help.

As the DC-3 descended to a thousand feet, Penny eased to the edge of the large cargo door and looked out onto the vast Montana landscape. Looking down on the pastoral scene, it was hard to believe that only minutes away, a towering blaze six miles across was moving twenty miles an hour, in the process killing everything in its path.

Penny saw the red light above the door begin to blink as he picked the headset off the hook. "Five minutes out, Penny," announced the pilot. "Coming in from the southeast. Winds are steady at five."

Penny felt his stomach drop as the plane descended under him. "Stand by!" he shouted above the wind noise to the nine other jumpers who were slowly getting to their feet, laboring under the heavy bulky gear. Penny took the headset off and put it back on the hook. "Hook up!" he shouted.

The group of jumpers fell in line, clipping their static lines onto the steel cable that ran the length of the plane overhead. Penny snapped in his own link and quickly secured his helmet, making sure the steel mesh facemask was secure. The last thing he needed going down through the trees in full gear was a stick through the face. As the plane leveled off he now stood stock still watching for the blinking red light to turn green.

A half-mile below, standing on the edge of the expansive meadow, Pearson pulled the pin on the red-colored smoke grenade and watched as the silver DC-3 lined up on the center of the DZ. He nodded to the other two firefighters who also held smoke grenades at the ready. "Okay!" he shouted. "Here they come. Light em up, boys."

Chapter Thirty

The Third and Fifth Corps of the Red Army counter attack started just before dawn. It was a thunderous artillery barrage that lasted well over an hour and was followed by a massive assault of flag-waving, mostly unarmed Russian troops. The Russian artillery had been ineffective, most of the rounds falling short. The infantry assault now in progress over open ground was being cut to pieces by precise German artillery and dug-in tank support. Hans watched in amazement from behind a thick earthen berm as large swaths of Russian troops, left unarmed by chronic weapon shortages were blown to ragged bits by German tank fire before even coming in rifle range. In Hans' mind, it was more of a planned slaughter than a battle, a large-scale suicide in the name of Soviet nationalism.

Mueller walked up, a half-lit cigarette dangling from his lips, carrying a pair of binoculars. "What the hell is wrong with these people?" he shouted above the thunderous tank fire. "They must be drunk; they're attacking across open ground!"

Hans took the binoculars and looked across the expansive valley at the growing carnage. "Fanatics," he replied, shaking his head as he handed the glasses back. "That's why they are so goddamned dangerous."

Mueller looked through the glass at the growing slaughter, amazed by the lack of any tactical gains in the human wave attack. He had heard stories from the old timers who had fought in the trenches during the Great War, stories about French human wave attacks, tales of German machinegun barrels melting down. All the while the wave of soldiers kept coming. Now, seeing it for himself, he was stunned by the imagery, the loss of life beyond description - madness.

Thirty minutes after the initial assault, dead and dying littered the field like hundreds of torn bloody rags. Survivors moved in groups of twos and threes, limping back under a grey haze of smoke and ash.

With nothing else to see, Mueller headed back to his tent with the unanswered question of "Why' echoing in his head. There would be no answer.

**

Just before midnight, as Hans set his watch beside a Tiger tank dug in behind a heavy berm, the thin frame of Lieutenant Snider appeared out of the darkness. Startled by the man's quiet approach, Hans instinctively raised his rifle and almost pulled the trigger. "It's Lieutenant Snider, Sergeant."

"Jesus," hissed Hans, angry at being surprised. "That's a good way to get shot, Lieutenant."

"Sorry. Any movement?"

"Other than German officers?"

Snider chuckled. "Other than German officers."

"No, sir. Just a few flares as the Reds collect some of the wounded."

Snider lit a cigarette, cupping the glowing red ember so as not to be seen. "I can only imagine what this place is like in the winter," he announced looking up into the moonless sky.

Hans thought for a moment trying to figure out what Snider was getting to. In the last three weeks of the offensive neither had spoken more than three words to the other. Now, Snyder felt the need to carry on a conversation - the last thing Hans wanted in the last hour of his watch. He did not like the young officer, nor did he trust him. To Hans, Snyder was a career climber, a tourist on his way up and out to bigger and better things. Being a part of the army and going to war was just another check in the box on his way up the ladder.

As Hans scanned the darkness, watching the flares go up a half-mile away on the Russian front lines, he smiled at the thought of how easy it would be to kill the young officer. His bayonet was razor sharp. A couple of deep slashes across the throat would have him bleeding out in minutes. It would be easy. He could blame the whole thing on Russian sappers who had crawled in and knifed the young officer as he walked around in the dark. He fingered the handle of his knife, feeling almost giddy with excitement at the prospect of killing the German. No one would know - a murder most perfect.

Just as he was about to give into that strange warm rage in the pit of his gut, Snyder spoke up and Hans pushed the dagger back in its scabbard. "Well, it looks like neither one of us will have to see this place in the winter."

Hans looked over at the silhouette of the young officer. "And why is that, sir?" he asked, still hanging onto the bloody fantasy.

"The Battalion is being pulled off the line. We have new orders. Just received the dispatch about three hours ago."

Hans took off his helmet and vigorously rubbed his scalp. "Are we in some kind of trouble?"

Snyder laughed. "No, on the contrary. The Battalion's performance throughout this campaign is being rewarded. We are heading to the desert under General Rommel's command, North Africa to be exact. Should be interesting."

Hans thought for a moment, surprised by the news. He had heard of Rommel, knew he was admired by the men in his command, known for being tough but fair. He was probably the best tactical officer in the German Army.

Hans smiled, liking the idea of seeing the desert. Any place was better than the Eastern Front. "So, when do we leave this shit hole?"

Snyder took a deep drag on the smoke and then snuffed it out in the berm. "Four days. Transport is on the way. Have a good night, Sergeant," announced Snyder slowly walking away into the gloom. "Thought you would want to know what was coming."

Hans put his helmet back on still digesting the news of the move. Watching the officer disappear in the dark, he dug the last two meth pills out of his shirt pocket and washed them down with the warm water from his canteen. He was doing all he could to stay awake; sleep was when the nightmares started. Holding on to knowing what was real and what was not was now taking real effort. With sleep, the dead came back and the spiders were as big as dogs. Killing Snyder just would have added one more to the hundreds he already saw when he closed his eyes. Maybe things would change in the desert, dry him out, kill the sickness. And then again, maybe there, in another moonless night on post, another officer unable to sleep would appear. He just might use the bayonet just to see if it calmed the storm - maybe.

***

It was now going on twenty-seven hours since Penny and the rest of his eight-man team had stepped out the door of the DC-3 into the biggest wildfire of Montana timber any of them had ever seen. Three times they had been flanked by the constantly changing winds that whipped the wall of flames in their direction, the heat nearly combusting their clothing as they ran for their lives. Every fire line frantically dug and every tree dropped in an attempt to starve the beast of fuel had failed, pushing the exhausted team farther into the mountains and further away from help.

Now, with fire on three sides, the team scrambled down a narrow ravine, crashing through the underbrush as panicked wild-eyed deer sprinted and jumped past them. Near the bottom, a narrow, waist-deep spur of the East Fork River slowly moved through the rocks and brush. "Hit the water!" shouted Penny from the rear of the group. "It's our only chance." As the men tumbled and splashed into the river, the last rays of sun slowly faded out, the dancing light from the fires reflecting in the water a brilliant orange.

"Jesus Christ!" shouted one of the men as he stumbled through the water. "We're gonna die!" Just then, off to the team's right, a seventy-foot blue spruce that had stood for fifty years exploded, its sap from trunk to tip super-heated by the surrounding sixty-foot wall of flames. The exploding tree sent foot-long shards of wood and embers in all directions like shrapnel from a bomb. Burned, beaten, and beyond exhausted, the men continued to stumble and slog their way down river as the pervasive west wind suddenly shifted again, giving the beleaguered team a brief respite. The river grew deeper and wider, allowing the men to float. Penny along with the rest dropped axes, shovels, and helmets, focusing now on not drowning, no easy feat in heavy logging boots and clothing.

Having moved a mile downstream after what seemed like hours of effort, the men slowly crawled out of the water one by one, the fire raging up the canyon behind them. As Penny lay exhausted in the dark. The rich, heavy smell of the reeds and mud mingling with wood smoke hung thick in the night air.

They had survived, barely escaping with only the singed clothing on their backs. Penny did a quick head count as he slowly got to his feet, relieved to see that all eight of his scorched and battered team members were still with the living. The fire had taken everything but their lives.

It had taken something more from Penny, something of great value that he had always taken for granted. In the three years of fighting big timber fires, he had never been beaten like this. His run to the river had been one of sheer panic, total fear in the face of something that demanded respect. Like the ocean, fire simply exists, caring nothing of the courage and strength of men. If the power is respected – you live. Ignore its strength and you die. Penny would never lose that respect again.

As he followed the team through the smoky darkness on the way back to the fire camp, no one said a word. What they had just endured had burned all the words away.

"Each man's work will become evident; for the day will show it because it is to be revealed with fire, and the fire itself will test the quality of each man's work."

1ˢᵗ Corinthians 3:13

Chapter Thirty-One

Just as the Mediterranean sun was cresting in the east, the German Krieg marine troop transport the *Goya,* carrying five hundred soldiers, slowly began an easy drift into the Tripoli harbor. Hans along with two hundred other SS troops from the battalion were finishing up their breakfast of coffee and hard rolls and beginning to make their way to the deck.

Even at this early hour he was already sweating heavily through the uniform shirt as he walked up to the rail, watching the countless white painted walls and red roofs of the city grow closer. It was a sprawling city with thousands of small houses and shops spilling right down to the water's edge. The warm air was filled with a mixture of aromas from early morning cooking fires, salt water, and a spice that Hans didn't recognize.

Now, less than two hundred meters away, it became apparent that the expansive dock was alive with activity as hundreds of porters and loaders began to gather carts and small wagons in preparation for the unloading of supplies and men. On board, the German deckhands quickly pulled thick ropes and cleats from the bow holes in a flurry of activity, the first mate shouting orders through a small megaphone on the rail from three decks above.

Hans watched in amusement as the chaos of shouting men and baying donkeys only intensified on the dock as the ship slowly eased toward the moorings. Lines were cast, gangways were lowered, and the organized melee of getting off the ship began. Hans, carrying his duffel bag filled with uniforms and clothes, clothes he doubted he would ever wear, and his weapon, joined the slow-moving line of men making their way down the long wooden gangway to the dock below.

Prior to the trip, desert uniforms had been issued, yellowish tan-colored shirts and wide leg shorts that made them look like pale-skin safari guides. Hans hated the shorts, and they would be the first thing to go once he got settled in. He was embarrassed by the paleness of his legs and could already hear snickers and laughter from the dark mass of dockworkers that were now furiously loading the ship supplies onto their backs and carts. As he reached the dock, one of the porters roughly grabbed Hans' duffle bag, attempting to stack it on the already heavily laden wagon. Hans jerked the bag back with one hand, swinging his rifle with the other. The barrel struck the man flush on the side of his head dropping him like a stone.

"Keep your hands off me, you fucking pigmy!" he shouted standing over the unconscious porter, his face red with rage. He kicked the man in the face. The only people laughing now were several fellow platoon members who were quickly pushing him away from the scene. The mood on the dock changed dramatically as the rest of the SS moved off the ship, parting the crowd like water, and onto the trucks waiting further up the street. A visceral message had been sent; the men in the tan shorts were not to be taken lightly – *do so at your own peril.*

For Hans, who now settled onto the hard wooden bench in the back of the open truck, that's exactly the kind of message he wanted to send. He wasn't here to help anyone;

he was here to kill people. In his mind one stranger was just as good a target as another.

"Welcome to Africa," announced Mueller smiling as he handed him a cigarette. "Nothing like making a first impression."

Hans laughed while lighting the smoke. "Nothing but fresh meat to me, my friend."

Mueller took off his cap, vigorously rubbing his scalp as the truck slowly made way through the crowded noisy street. "You know, we're going to die here!" he shouted half seriously, shaking his head.

Hans took a long drag and smiled, blowing the smoke out his nose. "Yeah, I know," he replied flicking the butt over the side. "There are worse places to die."

Mueller studied his friend's impassive face for a moment and then let the conversation die. "Jesus," he whispered to himself, feeling an odd sensation of coldness flash through his heart. He had made the comment in jest, hoping on some subconscious level, that he would get some kind of reassurance that they would *not* die in this God forsaken place. Instead he had gotten back a look of total fatal resignation, a look that chilled him to the bone. *Jesus* indeed.

***

Two months had passed since the big burn in that fateful season of Forty-one, and by the middle of October the first signs of winter were beginning to settle into the Bitterroot. Early mornings now carried a cold edge that fogged the breath and cast a familiar light, an angle of shadows that announced to the subconscious that summer was over and a major change was on the way.

In the rest of country, the Yankees' DiMaggio had extended his hitting streak to 57 games. The Les Brown song of Jolt'in Joe DiMaggio played non-stop on the radio in celebration of the accomplishment. Bread had gone up to eight cents a loaf. Milk had hit an all-time high of thirty-five cents a gallon. Penny and the rest of the crew had noticed the spike at the Sula store where they bought their groceries during the summer, chalking it up to the bad news in Europe about the growing war.

With the fire season over most of the team had drifted back into the part-time jobs in Missoula that kept them warm during the winter, a cycle now familiar. They became short order cooks, bartenders, and snow removal experts in the winter, a profound transformation for hard men who stepped out of airplanes to fight raging forest fires in the summer.

Pearson had worked his influence with the Director of Forestry in Washington that fall and had been able to secure a caretaker position for Penny for the rest of the year. He would stay on the government payroll, responsible for maintaining fire crew equipment and facilities not only at Seeley Lake but three other fire camps near the Idaho border. For Penny, anything was better than bartending down at the Moose Lodge in town. He would not miss the smell of stale beer, cigarette smoke, and grease coming from the grill, nor the drunken miners, half-crazed cowboys who had been alone far too long, or the fast talking greasy-haired land speculators who drifted in and out of the bars and hotels all winter. Outside in the mountains, even in the cold weather, was the only place he really wanted to be. It was home, his home, the one place in the world where his heart settled and his mind cleared.

By middle November he had settled into a working routine that had him driving the snow and slush-covered backroads all the way up to the Sealy Lake station and back through the now closed fire camps along the East Fork River, a route that took a solid seven hours to complete. Deer and elk hunters were the people he now ran across on most on his checks, men feeding their families with the game they hunted.

He checked the camp structures, making sure they were not vandalized or occupied by squatters. As winter tightened its grip and the snow grew deeper on the passes and backroads, he began spending a good bit more time drinking coffee and talking to the locals at the Montana Café down in Darby. More often than not, Darby was about as far as he could go due to the worsening road conditions.

The setting sun was little more than a reddish purple light behind the Saw Tooth Mountains one early evening in November as he turned off the gravel road that linked the Sealy Lake station to the highway leading back to Missoula. Turning on his headlights, he thought about all the things he had seen since that terrible day on his porch in Kansas three years ago. He caught his reflection in the truck mirror as he drove. Even though a lifetime of experiences had toughened his body and hardened his soul he could still see the same scared, skinny kid that had carried the battered suitcase and worn an overcoat two sizes too big, the kid who had killed a man within hours of running away from home. He lit a cigarette, tossing the burnt match out the truck window into the snow, letting the cold mountain air blow out the memory of that terrible day.

What would he change if he could, he thought. What if God himself came down from heaven, sat in the seat beside him, and asked him that very question? What would he say? He missed his parents, but their memory no longer brought a tear, only a dull fleeting pain to the heart, a pain that left as quickly as it came. He missed his friend and mentor Mitch, a man who somehow had recognized his potential and given him the most incredible opportunity of his life. The memory of Mitch was one that did bring a tear, dropping a thick emotional blanket of melancholy on him that lasted hours, sometimes days. That was something he would change if he could. He would look the Almighty right in His eye and tell him to bring Mitch back. He had been too good of a man to die the way he did. It just had seemed too soon, way too soon.

Three weeks later on December seventh on a beautiful cloudless Sunday morning, the Imperial Japanese Navy sent three quarters of the US Navy Fleet to the muddy bottom of Pearl Harbor, Hawaii, killing over twenty-five-hundred sailors and civilians. Three days after that, Penny drove down to the small recruiting office in Missoula, raised his right hand, and enlisted in the Army. The war had finally found him. Everything was about to change.

"Cry havoc and let slip the dogs of war!" **Julius Caesar**

Chapter Thirty-Two

"So, what exactly is our mission here?" asked Mueller sitting up in the large open window as a hot desert breeze blew in, a breeze that made the sweltering room even hotter. Hans, shirtless and coated in sweat, sat in front of a slow moving fan. He had just come from an NCO meeting at the newly erected camp headquarters which was in reality a dilapidated villa and crumbling walled compound that had once been the palatial estate and vineyards of a French diplomat back in the twenties. The only other inhabitants in the area, a population of ten thousand, resided in the dust-colored town of Oran several miles to the east. It had taken eight hours by truck for Hans' unit to get to the camp from the port, a brutal, bone-jarring trip in the hot sun and talcum-like dust that had put everyone into a state of weary edginess.

Hans lit a cigarette as a drop of sweat dripped off his nose onto the smoke. "Evidently we are here to train and assist the Algerian and French Vichy forces occupying this area," replied Hans wiping the sweat from his face. "From what I've seen, these bastards, a bunch of shit heels in uniform, need all the help they can get."

Mueller laughed. "So you're not impressed with our comrades in arms?"

"Shit," snorted Hans, "we would be doing the shits a favor if we lined them all up and machined-gunned the lot - useless."

Mueller looked out over the desolate desert landscape. The only life he could see was a small herd of skinny goats grazing on what little scrub brush and nettle weeds they could find fifty yards away. A young boy who looked to be no more than ten slowly walked among the animals with a long stick, prodding and pushing the herd. The sound of a small cow bell on one of the goats drifted on the hot desert wind.

"I like it here," announced Mueller watching the boy. "It's peaceful."

Frustrated, Hans flipped the switch on the fan several times trying to make it spin faster to no avail. "It's a goddamned furnace. I don't know how anyone survives in this heat."

"Still better than the Eastern Front," replied Mueller pulling off his shirt to let the warm air cool the sweat on his neck and chest. "If I never see the mud of Mother Russia again, it would suit me just fine."

Hans sat back in his chair and poured the rest of the warm water from his canteen over his head and face. Looking to the ceiling, he blew a spray and then wiped his nose. "Let's see if you still feel that way after six months," he announced.

Mueller looked back out to the goat herd now moving through a shallow ravine. *You can't ruin this for me,* he said to himself, *not this time.*

***

For Penny, the transition from the Forestry Service Smoke Jumper program to the military was an easy one. The regimentation, the clear-cut emphasis on predictable order was familiar, almost comforting. He had rested emotionally in the routine and stability the Army had offered almost from day one. Oddly enough, it felt like home. It was a place he could stay as long as he wanted and the rewards of his physical effort would be bestowed.

He completed the six weeks of basic training at Fort Leonard Wood, Missouri, while hardly breaking a sweat, having arrived in peak condition from Montana. The predawn runs, the calisthenics were nothing compared to the rigors of working for years at altitude in the mountains. Two days after graduation, he was on a Piedmont bus headed for Fort Benning, Georgia, with a fresh set of orders assigning him to the newly formed 509th Airborne Infantry Regiment (PIR). General William Lee from the original Parachute Platoon, had been keeping tabs from afar, making sure that Penny was immediately assigned to Airborne status upon graduation from Basic. In addition, he had been promoted to Corporal, something unheard of for someone who had only been in the Army six weeks.

In addition to his new rank, he would be the only United States Army Paratrooper who did not have to attend Basic Airborne training at Fort Benning. He arrived at his new duty station in Georgia with already more parachute jumps than any man in the unit, including the senior NCOs, an odd fact that gave him immediate status in the regiment and a heightened curiosity about his background among the troops.

Even though he had been asked about his family upon his arrival at the unit, he had kept his answers vague, deflecting the conversations back to Montana and his life as a Smoke

Jumper. He saw no gain in revealing the hard-edged details of his father's death, nor did he want even a whisper of suspicion directed his way concerning the shooting in the box car. No matter how much he rationalized in his mind that the shooting was self-defense, he had killed a man and the memory of that terrible night haunted him to the core. He knew instinctively that somewhere a greater power was keeping score of all the things, both the good and the decidedly bad he had done in his life, things that needed to be brought to the cold-eye of judgment, a history that demanded justice - atonement.

That night, as he stood in the large shower room of the barracks drying himself off, he thought about his father. What would he have to say about the path his life had taken? The question hung in the air like the wispy steam of the showers, unanswered as it always had been.

"Jesus, Corporal," announced Melvin Biddle, a skinny nineteen-year-old Private from Indiana who had just graduated from Jump School. "How did you get that scar on your back?" Penny wrapped the towel around his neck and glanced at the lightning scar reflected in the bank of mirrors above the twelve sinks in the large room.

Across the room twelve commodes sat side by side without partitions in between, the Army's none-too-subtle way of putting everyone on the same level. You slept together in two-story, forty-man open bays, ate together in the mess hall, ran together in platoon formation, showered together in large open room showers, and at the end of the day sat next to your buddy and took a shit together. As one of Penny's drill instructors had said, "If the Army had wanted you to have privacy, they would have issued it to you."

"I got hit by lightning," he replied walking past Biddle. It had been the first time in years that anyone had brought up the question of how he got the large tree-shaped scar on his back, an incident he never really thought about much, maybe because the strike was so close to the life he had lived prior to Montana, a time of desperate wandering and fear, a time of feeling lost - a bad time.

"No shit?" replied Biddle, wanting to hear more. "My Aunt Bell got hit by lightning a couple years ago hanging up sheets. Killed her dead as a hammer right there in her back yard." The young Private seemed very excited about his discovery and obviously wanted to talk about it more. "Hell, you must be the luckiest son-of-a-bitch in the world, Corporal."

Penny smiled while pulling on his T-shirt. "Yea, maybe," he replied starting to walk out of the shower room. The past was something he definitely didn't want to talk about. "It was a long time ago. Don't remember much about it." It was a lie of course; he remembered every agonizing second.

The kid laughed and tossed his canvas shaving kit and towel into one of the sinks and extended his hand. "Name's Biddle, Corporal. Everybody in the Company calls me Melvin, all except Sergeant Ross. He calls me "shit for brains."

Penny laughed and shook hands. "Penny Reynolds. Pleased to meet ya, Melvin," He liked the kid immediately.

Biddle, who seemed to be a walking ball of barely constrained energy, paused in thought for a moment and then quickly walked over to the row of commodes, dropped his pants, and began a loud farting crap. He looked up at Penny with a broad smile. "Ain't army chow great?"

Penny laughed while walking out of the room shaking his head. "Jesus, Melvin."

Little did he know that three years after their first meeting, Melvin Biddle would receive the Congressional Medal of Honor for valor during the invasion of Sicily. He would live a long full life after the war, marry his high school sweetheart, have two wonderful daughters, then die of heart failure in 2010 at the age of eighty-seven, buried in his hometown of Anderson, Indiana.

"In war there are no unwounded soldiers"

Jose Norask

Chapter Thirty-Three

As early as May of Forty-two, the Allies were planning the invasion of North Africa. Tunisia, Algiers, and Morocco were all targets for what was to be a decisive push to end the Axis' hold in the area. For a year now, General Rommel and his famed Afrika Korps had been slamming the British forces in bloody skirmishes and predawn fire fights and then fading into the endless desert only to hit days later with sledgehammer force on the unprotected British flanks' desperately needed supply lines, hence the title the "Desert Fox," a moniker Rommel personally disliked.

Both the German and the Allied forces now recognized that they were locked into a mutually destructive blood feud, one that had become a nightmarish war of attrition. Allied Command had designed Operation Torch to end the vicious stalemate. It would be a joint operation with both American ground and Airborne units working together to secure the harbors and airfields throughout the Axis advance. Months prior to the operation, Penny's entire 509th Airborne Regiment had been sent to Halifax, England, for staging.

After a thirteen-day float across the Atlantic, just after dawn on September 5, 1942, Penny hoisted his forty-pound duffel bag onto his shoulder along with his M1 rifle and started down the long gangway from the six-story troop ship USS West Point to the crowded dock in Halifax. A light rain had begun to fall adding a chill to the already adrenaline charged air and a muted shade to the early morning light, not quite sunshine yet not quite overcast - classic English weather for this time of year.

Looking down the long switch-back gangplank, Penny watched the slow moving line of OD green helmeted men inch towards the dock, their helmets carrying a dull gloss from the rain. He was glad to be moving, relieved to be away from the countless pools of seasick vomit, the incredibly cramped sleeping conditions, and the pervasive smell of diesel fumes. As he walked, he filled his lungs with the salt-scented air, feeling better by the minute. This entire month had been a month of firsts - first time on a ship, first time traveling out of the country, first war.

He knew what was expected of him, had accepted the position of squad leader knowing full well that the six young men in his squad would be looking to him for guidance, guys only a year or two younger than him, a fact not lost on any of them. They had come from small towns across the country, small rural bergs most people had never heard of - Havre, Montana; Greenbow, Kentucky; Anderson, Indiana, places that moved to their own rhythm, providing a pace of life rich in its slowness and routine, narrow in its vision. For the young - a place to be from, rarely a destination.

If Penny had been able to see the future that cold wet morning a million miles away from everything he knew, he would have never gotten off the boat. Young men were soon going to die in places most people had never heard of - Kasarine Pass, Tobrok, Barcia : places that moved to their own ancient rhythm, places rich in a history that would soon be written in the blood of thousands.

In less than twenty days he would kill for the second time in his life, all actions sanctioned and blessed by the gods of war. His only task was to try and live through it all. At the moment, it was all a casual coin toss by the shot callers. Some things never change... never.

***

Hans had been watching the buzzards high overhead slowly drifting on the hot wind thermals for most of the afternoon. Watching the heat shimmer in the distance, he sat in the open top jeep, stripped down to his boots, uniform shorts, and undershirt trying to decide if the now rotting cow lying on the edge of the desolate airstrip would be a hazard to landing aircraft. By the look of it, the birds had been at it all morning, making a proper mess of the carcass. He took a deep drink from the warm water in his canteen watching several of the large black vultures settle on the cow in a flutter of wings and loud squawking. A faint, hot gust of wind carried the smell of rotting meat in his direction ending the debate. He was not about to move the mess. If the supply plane could not land because of a rotting dead cow on the edge of the runway, so be it.

He started the jeep, dropped it into gear, and headed out into the desert for no other reason than he was bored and just needed to be moving. Driving into the desolate landscape to see nothing had become his routine. Being the junior NCO at the camp meant he was the one responsible for rotating the guards through watch, making sure the vehicles used to pick up supplies were maintained, and any other shit-job the highers did not want.

So far the only training his unit had done with the Algerians had been a joint rifle range practice which had consisted of SS shooting and zeroing weapons and then standing back to watch the Algerians miss the targets, drop their weapons, and generally fuck-up for the rest of the afternoon. Several times the German range masters had offered to help with the shooting only to be waved off by the Algerian officers.

At the end of the day the Algerian's consensus was that the SS were a bunch of arrogant pricks that cared nothing for anyone but themselves. From the Germans point of view - the Algerians were low-life cannon-fodder, subhuman meat targets that would be the first to die if and when the shooting started.

There was a pride issue involved, a cultural barrier of mistrust that would take concerted effort on both sides to cross. For Hans the issue had been settled weeks ago. If any of his dark-skin comrades got in his way, he would shoot them to pieces without a second thought. The only real soldiers stationed at the compound were the SS. Every other person was just an armed tourist and nothing more.

After driving a solid three miles out into the desert, he stopped the jeep and let the silence of the openness wrap around him like a hot blanket. To the west - Morocco, to the north across the cool blue Mediterranean- Spain, to the east -Libya, and to the south - Mali and the lawless Chad where the Spanish Saharan bandits gave no mercy to anyone they came across yet prayed to God five times a day. Hans had heard the stories of heavily armed SS patrols heading into that wasteland only to be never heard from or seen again. It was all ghost story bullshit as far as he was concerned. There was no way any of these backward bush-shitters could take down an SS unit…impossible.

He scanned the horizon with his binoculars entertaining the fantasy of picking up his weapon and the half empty canteen and heading north until he was knee-deep in the Mediterranean. He'd throw his weapon in the surf, and lie in the sun, and drink beer until all the dark visions went away.

Suddenly, overhead, at some distance, he picked up the sound of a plane he had not heard before, a deep droning hum that drifted in and out of the hot breeze gusting around the jeep. After scanning the sky with his binoculars for several minutes, he spotted the plane and immediately felt a bolt of excitement hit just above the heart. His best guess, the aircraft was flying at about three thousand feet and carried the distinctive outline of an Allied DC-3.

As if having a sense of being watched, the plane slowly gained altitude, made a wide slow left hand turn, and then headed back in the direction from which it had come. Hans watched the plane until it disappeared in the haze knowing instinctively that what he had just seen was important. He knew that this was a reconnaissance aircraft at the very least. Something was in the works. His instincts, honed by years of facing life and death situations where events developed with nuance, whispered to him that things were about to change. It was a jarring realization that the Allies were within striking distance, maybe in mass, something that had seemed impossible until now.

Finally, he thought quickly starting the jeep almost giddy with excitement; he was going to get back into the war, back into what he had joined the SS for in the first place. He could not stop smiling as he pushed the jeep to go as fast as it would across the desert on his way back to the compound. Maybe the gods of war really had heard his prayers. Maybe.

In Arabic there is a word for storm – *Khamsin*, a wind mass that originates in the cool waters off the southern Mediterranean and pushes southwest where it collides with the hot, dry desert air coming off the sub-Saharan coast. On occasion, the result is a windstorm of Biblical intensity. One such storm was even recorded by Napoleon in his conquest of the Middle East, a storm so intense that it lasted three days and buried horses in sand up to the bridle while suffocating hundreds of his troops as they huddled in tents and makeshift dugouts. It had taken four days to dig his bewildered and dazed army out of the sand.

It is rumored that the shepherds and herders who eke out a living in the vast nothingness of the sub-Sahara can smell a Khamsin coming. People who have studied the phenomena attribute the smell to the rising ozone levels, giving the air a similar scent to that of a pending rain storm. The smell is so widely trusted by the inhabitants of the area that it can trigger a mass exodus of herder and flock alike away from the high places and open ground and into protected canyons or structures to wait it out. For all the technology at the Allies disposal at the start of the North African campaign, nothing compared to the indigenous people's tribal knowledge concerning the weather, an asset ignored that would soon have a tremendous cost. Wind and sand were not the only things that would soon be blown away.

***

It had been two days since Hans had reported the Allied aircraft yet had been assured by the senior staff at the compound that the Luftwaffe had complete control of the air over all of North Africa and that he should be more concerned about doing his duty than wandering around in the desert. For Hans, the overconfident, condescending way in which his concerns were minimized made him even more suspicious that something was going on.

"Maybe you took too many pills. Maybe it was a hallucination," Mueller said, handing Hans the bottle of warm wine. They were sitting on one of the low stone walls that crisscrossed the compound, something they did on most nights after evening mess. A hazy moon cast a muted light across the landscape as the wind died just before sunset leaving the desert darkness hot and unusually still.

Hans popped another methamphetamine, Pervitin, into his mouth and chased it down with a deep drink of wine. He was doing all he could to contain the anger at basically being told to mind his own business and ignore his instincts, instincts that had been honed to a sharp edge by years of war and close-quarter battle.

"I know what I saw, Mueller," he replied tossing the empty bottle into the dark. "It was no hallucination. They know more than they are saying. I can feel it."

Mueller thought for a moment. Over the past month he had watched Hans grow increasingly bored and disgruntled about their new post. He had not adjusted to the slower pace or the heat. Nor had he accepted his new role as advisor to the French Algerian unit, openly viewing them as subhuman Cretans he had to deal with. He had noticed the damage done by the pills himself and had stopped taking them weeks ago. "I don't know, my friend. Even if it were the Allies, I doubt the Americans give a red piss about Africa." He pushed himself off the wall. "I'm going to sleep. That fucking wine gave me a headache. You should do the same. You look like shit."

Hans nodded and lit a cigarette as Mueller slowly made his way down the wall and then disappeared into the dark like a ghost. To hell with it, maybe he was making too much of it, he thought, shivering involuntarily as the meth started to kick in. The drug sent the now familiar cold rush that started at the top of his head and then rolled over his shoulders and chest like someone pouring ice cold water down the back of his neck. Aside from the nausea which usually went away within the hour, he enjoyed the feeling. His addiction to the pills had solidified; he could not imagine what life would be like without them.

Feeling energized, he pushed himself off the wall and flicked the acrid tasting Turkish cigarette out into the dark. He needed to walk and try to put the jumble of thoughts and images now racing through his head into some kind of logical order.

Recently Hans had noticed that his thoughts were more scattered while on the pills as opposed to the focus of his senses and emotions he had noted when he first started taking them. In the beginning he felt a clarity of purpose yet a controlled detachment. Now, as he walked through the stifling hot darkness, he was barely in control, the bubbling irrational rage just below the surface making him want to scream in fury. He pulled his razor sharp trench knife from the sheath as he walked, hoping, praying he would come across someone he could use it on. Maybe blood up to his elbows would quiet the noise in his head and the fire racing through his veins... maybe.

Little did he know that, in twenty-seven hours, the methamphetamine addiction and all that came with it would be the least of his problems. Out there in the dark, something even more dangerous than the storm was on the way, something that would change the world forever.

Chapter Thirty-Four

First Lieutenant Kyle Cooper of the 12th US Army Aircorp worked at keeping the DC-3 at a consistent altitude in conditions that were deteriorating by the minute. His plane was part of a squadron of six aircraft loaded with paratroopers from the 509th Airborne tasked with capturing the expansive German airfield near Oran, Algeria.

They were a small part of a much bigger mission involving both Allied air and ground forces code named Operation "**Torch**", the start of the Allied invasion of North Africa. In the operations briefing, Cooper, along with the other air crews, had been told that the weather over the Algerian coast might be rough but what he was starting to fly through now was becoming untenable. The crosswinds alone had to be moving at around thirty-knots, with visibility dropping rapidly. Cooper peered out into the darkness at the edge of the howling sand storm, and as he began to fly into it, he struggled to stay aloft as the plane dropped and then jolted skyward. Sand peppered the windshield. A strange high pitch whine was now coming through the engines.

Keying the radio, he quickly made his decision without even asking the copilot Mike Varner, a twenty-three-year-old second Lieutenant from Ohio, who looked terrified in the dim red glow of the cockpit lights. "Range Rider 26 to all flights. I am aborting my run. Repeat, I am aborting my run. The weather is closing us out. Do you copy?" The radio came alive with responses.

"Ah Roger that, Range Rider. This is Big Duke Seven," replied his wing man. "I'm at your three o'clock. I can't fly in this stuff either. Will be aborting on heading seventeen-niner. How do you copy?"

Before Cooper could reply, he felt a heavy dull thud reverberate through the left side of the aircraft that dropped his wing, putting him into a hard left turning dive. "Lost the engine!" shouted Varner trying desperately to re-fire the magneto from his side of the consul. Cooper retrieved the trim, temporarily stopping the turn and leveling off. He checked the altitude indicator, shocked to see he had dropped almost a thousand feet and had just missed colliding with Big Duke Seven by less than three hundred feet.

"Son-of-a-bitch," he said flipping on the green jump command light, knowing it was their only chance. They were far too heavy. "Get em out now before we lose the other engine!" he shouted through his radio, fighting the yoke for control.

"Jesus Christ!" shouted Verner on the verge of tears, doing everything he could to re-fire the engine as the plane took another sickening dip.

"We're going down, Mike. Get them out now! You too!" shouted Cooper struggling with the controls. "I don't know how much longer I can hold it."

Verner ripped off his lap and shoulder harness and tossed his headset on the consul. "What about you, Coop?" he shouted climbing out of his seat.

"Get out now, Mike. Get those guys out of here! Move!" It was the last time either man saw or spoke to the other.

Penny knew the second the DC-3 took a hard dip and turn that the aircraft and everyone in it were on borrowed time. He knew by the sound of the engines that the Douglas was going down and that there wasn't a thing anybody on board could do about it. Even before the copilot burst through the cockpit cabin door in a panic shouting for everyone to exit, he had gotten to his feet and opened the cargo door, now a howlingblack hole in the side of the airplane. Lieutenant Avery, the platoon commander, stunned by Penny's actions, grabbed him by the arm trying to stop him as Penny quickly hooked up his static line.

"What the hell do you think you're doing, Corporal? Sit down and wait for orders!" shouted Avery, struggling to stand up under his heavy combat load as the plane dropped and rose erratically. Penny jerked the officer up by the shoulders and in one quick move reached over his back and grabbed the snap link that was attached to his static line.

'The plane is going down, sir. You gotta jump now!" he shouted over the wind noise. "We gotta get out now!"

Avery grabbed the front of Penny's shirt and began screaming in his face, "I am in charge here, Corporal! Sit down! That's an order goddamnit!"

By now, the practically hysterical copilot had begun screaming for everyone to get out as the plane dropped out from under his feet and then rose again knocking him to his knees. Penny quickly snapped the protesting officer's link on to the overhead cable and with a running shove pushed the flaying officer out into the darkness.

He turned back to the rest of the men. "Let's go!" he shouted. Most were already standing, hooked up, and moving towards the door. Evidently, the only person who had not known that the plane was in real trouble had been Lieutenant Avery, who at this very moment, was drifting somewhere over North Africa.

Within seconds every man in the plane including the copilot had jumped into the darkness. Just before he stepped out into the howling void himself, Penny caught a quick glimpse through the cabin door of the pilot, the side of his face illuminated in the red glow of the cock pit lights as he fought for control to keep the plane aloft. It was the most selfless, brave thing he had ever seen a man do. In that moment, he knew that if he lived through this night, he would make sure the lone pilot was never forgotten... never.

***

It was just before dawn when large drifts of talc-fine sand covered the vehicles and buildings alike after the passing of the storm that the sirens of the German compound began to wail. Hans, having just fallen asleep, was jolted awake by the noise. He had no idea the sirens attached to several poles in the area were even hooked up much less why they were sounding. He grabbed his MP 40 machinegun and the leather pouch holding four extra magazines and headed out the door at a trot. An officer in his undershirt and uniform trousers pointed at Hans as he stepped outside his quarters. "Sergeant, load your squad in that truck and get to the airfield! It's under attack!" he shouted.

The compound was now a flurry of activity as half-dressed SS troops poured out of their quarters, pulling on gear as they began piling into the trucks and jeeps.

Mueller, fully dressed, ran up to Hans who was climbing into the passenger side of one of the trucks. "What's going on?" he shouted running along the now-moving vehicle.

"Get in the back!" yelled Hans, slamming the door. "We're under attack!"

Mueller turned, catching the end of the lorry. Several men in the back were reaching to pull him aboard just as a heavy mortar round slammed into the middle of the German compound, sending a spray of white-hot shrapnel and building plaster in all directions.

Hans glanced in the truck's side mirror just as a second and then a third mortar round landed in the compound behind them, the rounds impacted where he had stood just minutes before.

***

A distant popping sound, growing louder and closer, began to pull Penny from semi-consciousness. His eyes opened to see daylight. A small part of the white silk canopy was lazily blowing in the warm breeze and then collapsing, the rest of the chute in a bunched heap in and around a thick stand of knee-high weeds.

He could taste blood and, running his tongue over his gums painfully discovered that he had lost one of his front teeth and broken the other in half. Lying there in the ditch, he felt as if he had been hit by a car, remembering nothing of the landing. He slowly sat up, trying to shake the cobwebs from his head, and

The operational objective for his unit had been the German held airfield near the town of Orman. He and the rest of his platoon had bailed out of the crippled DC-3 at three thousand feet with a sixty mile-an-hour crosswind in a raging sand storm and appeared to have landed nowhere close to that objective. Brushing dried blood from his nose and sand from his eyes, he painfully got to his feet and, in stunned surprise, he looked down from the small rise onto the expansive German Airfield of Orman. They had been blown a solid ten to twelve miles across desert, dropping them almost exactly in the planned location – incredible.

Still in a daze, Penny watched as two then three American soldiers ran by. A firm hand suddenly gripped his shoulder. "Hey, buddy, you okay?"

He turned to the voice and saw the helmet - a big red cross in the white circle. "Jesus, you're part of that Airborne drop?" questioned the medic, pulling him down to the ground. We've been finding bodies from that craziness everywhere. Shit, you're the first one we've found alive. What's your name, pard?"

Penny shook his head. "Ah... Reynolds, Penny Reynolds from the 509th. Who are you?"

The young solider, who looked about twelve, handed him a canteen. "Private Casswell, First Division. We hit the beach last night. We just got here. Been pushing the Vichy and the krauts back since dawn. This air field is our objective. Looks like we beat em here."

Penny took a long drink of water and then handed the canteen back. "You said you found bodies? What did you mean? My guys were killed by the Germans?"

The medic put the canteen back in its pouch and picked up his large aid bag. "Naw, brother, more like contact with the ground. Like I said, you're the first guy I've seen alive from that group. Some of the folks look like they hit the ground doing sixty. Fucking Airborne, you guys have got to be nuts to jump out of a perfectly good airplane."

Penny gently touched his lip and the jagged edges of his remaining front tooth. "Wasn't so perfect last night," he replied, unbuckling his chest harness and leg straps, still trying to comprehend what was going on.

The medic leaned over and raised Penny's lip with his thumb, studying the damage. "Yeah, well looks like you took a good hit to the face. Busted some teeth. I've seen worse. Here's a couple aspirin." He pulled a small bottle of pills from his pocket. "That's all I can give ya; have to save the morphine for guys getting hit."

Penny swallowed the aspirin, wincing from the effort, his entire body beginning to ache.

"Anyway, good luck, Reynolds," announced the medic patting Penny on the shoulder. "I got to get down to my guys." He picked up his aid bag and trotted off down the slope. "Stay alive, Airborne!" he shouted over his shoulder. "Gonna be a long war."

Through the dust, off in the distance at the far end of the airfield, Penny could now see a column of transport trucks and jeeps rolling to a stop. He could actually see German soldiers unloading as the First Division troops opened up with heavy machine gun and mortar fire from his side of the field. Tracers from all directions zipped across the runway, skipping high in the sky like tiny meteors. As more soldiers from both sides arrived at the airfield, the battle intensified.

Staying low, he stripped off the rest of his jump gear and tore into the padded jump bag that held his rifle. To his shock, he found the weapon broken in half just behind the trigger assembly. "Son-of-a-bitch!" he shouted looking around trying to figure out what to do next. Here he was in the middle of a major battle, his first contact with the enemy, and he was unarmed. Rounds, now suddenly snapping the air a foot above his head, slammed into the edge of the ditch. Someone from the other side of the field had spotted him.

***

Hans watched as a full two companies of American troops swarmed over the low hills at the far end of the runway. Another large group, at least a hundred backed by two Sheridan tanks, moved up the narrow access road that ran the length of the airfield. The two light Luftwaffe supply bombers parked on the far side by the hangers for the last two days were now on fire.

Mueller dropped down beside him and began firing a MG 42 machinegun at the middle of the American assault four hundred meters away. Mortar rounds now dropping in and around the German position were causing heavy casualties with each impact.

"We can't hold them!" shouted Mueller frantically loading another belt of ammo in the MG. "There's too many!" In all the years, in all the battles they had fought together, Hans had never seen the intensity of fear now etched deeply in his friend's face. In that brief terrifying moment when their eyes met, something profound passed between them, an unspoken communication, an acknowledgement that their lives were over, that they would not walk away from this fight. It would all end here.

For Hans, when that final truth became evident, he had an odd calm, a strange almost euphoric feeling of awareness and peace. This is how he wanted to die. This was the honorable reward for warrior service to the Fatherland. This would be remembered. He patted Mueller on the shoulder and motioned that he was moving left. Mueller nodded, quickly reloading the last belt of machinegun ammunition just as another mortar round crashed in thirty yards behind them, the shrapnel whizzing over their heads.

***

Penny looked behind him as another company of First Division troops moved down the road to join the battle for the airfield. Three hundred yards away, the Germans were now beginning to retreat in small groups only to be shot down by the vastly superior numbers. The bloody route became even deadlier as two P40 Tomahawk American fighters came in low and fast off the desert horizon, their twin fifties ripping trucks, jeeps. and the remaining Germans forces to pieces. Penny watched in awe as the slaughter continued, some of the Germans standing their ground only to be blasted apart by the fighters and the advancing troops. Seeing his opportunity, he jumped up from his position in the ditch and ran to the back of an advancing column of fresh troops and tanks that were now moving up the narrow road that ran from the town of Orman to the airfield.

As he crouch-walked behind the group, he felt naked – weaponless. The fighters roared by overhead making another deadly strafing run. Off to his left he suddenly spotted a badly wounded American lying in a pool of blood, having been hit low in the belly. A medic was already crouched beside him doing what he could to keep the man alive. As he walked by, Penny picked up the dying soldier's M1 still slick with blood. He pulled the cocking handle as he continued to walk and saw that the mag well was full.

Smoke from the burning vehicles now hung heavy in the hot desert air as the last of the German resistance dropped off to single rifle shots followed by a responding fusillade of rifle and machinegun fire. No quarter was being given.

***

Hans, crouching as low as he could in the drainage ditch bordering the far left side of the runway, ejected the machinegun's empty magazine and loaded the last one from the pouch. Still unscathed from the fight, he knew he was one of the few remaining men from his unit. He slowly peered over the ditch bank at the advancing Americans now less than a hundred yards away. The ground vibrated, announcing the approaching tanks. This was going to be it. With sweat running into his eyes and the desert dirt smell close to his face, he realized that these were the last sensations he would have on this earth. He would wait until they were nearly on top of him and then open fire, taking as many as he could with him. As the sounds of troops and tanks grew closer, he found himself counting breaths, letting the last few seconds of his life drift away in the heat.

***

Fifty yards ahead of him, Penny watched as two tanks leading the column took a slow left turn and stopped. Feeling exposed at the edge of the runway, he trotted over to a small ditch and, to his stunned surprise, landed nearly on top of a crouching German soldier. For a brief second the men locked eyes, the shock of the encounter freezing them both in place, open-mouthed. In slow motion, Penny watched as the German raised his machinegun from the hip and fired from two feet away. A fraction of a second before the weapon went off, Penny dove headlong into the German, his helmet deflecting three of the four nine-millimeter rounds, the fourth bullet ripping into his shoulder just above the collar bone and exiting his back just below his left shoulder blade, a wound he did not feel.

The German slammed to the ground and lost consciousness as Penny rained down a flurry of haymaker punches that left the soldier bloody. Hearing the gunfire, several other GIs jumped down into the ditch and pulled him off the German.

"Holy shit!" shouted one of the men holding Penny down. "You just captured one of them SS assholes! I'll be dammed, boy!" Laughing, he pulled Penny to his feet. "You want me to shoot this son-of-a-bitch for ya?" he asked, pointing his weapon at the man.

Still breathing heavily, Penny kicked the machinegun out of the reach of the German who had begun to come around. "No, he might have valuable intel," he announced kneeling down to pull the man's trench knife out of his belt. "He's now a prisoner. We're taking this one alive."

He stood up, a dull ache radiating through his left side and up the back of his neck. He began to have a hard time breathing, his vision growing dark. A concerned look on the face of the soldier that had run to his side was the last thing he saw and then…nothing at all as he collapsed on top of the German. For Corporal Pendleton Reynolds, 1st Battalion, Company C/509th Airborne, the war was over.

"For not by numbers of men, nor by measure of body, but by valor of soul is war to be decided." —Belisarius

Chapter Thirty-Five

Yesterday............

An article about Smoke Jumpers was a story that had been drifting through the cluttered archives of his mind for some time now. The parachuting aspect was interesting, yet the real draw for him was the connection to Montana, the Sealy Lake area in particular.

Cliff Gibson had worked for the "Missoulian" as a feature writer for the last 15 years, a job he had taken right out of Penn State Journalism School as an excuse to live in Montana. On his first trip to the state, he took a four-pound rainbow out of the East Fork and the hook might as well have gone into him. The following summer he had packed everything he had and headed west without a second thought. As far as he was concerned, it had been the best move he had ever made.

Fifteen years later, with Veterans Day only weeks away, he was looking for a story. The lead editor had been sending him emails all week asking for a local piece about still-living local Vets who had served in World War Two.

Through a little research, he had discovered a man living just outside of Darby who had earned the Distinguished Service Cross and had been involved somehow with the early Smoke-Jumper program back in its early days. As far as Gibson was concerned that combination might be a good story. It would at least get Thompson, the editor, off his back.

By Thursday of that week Gibson had punched in the Darby Community Center address on the GPS and pointed his truck down Highway 93 toward the Sula area. A light rain followed him out of town but soon cleared as he passed through Stevensville. It was late October and the cold air had already come down from the Saw Tooth Mountains and would hang on till spring. Winter came early and stayed late this far north. He pulled into the Darby community center parking lot by noon and made contact with the elderly woman at the desk. He knew her name was Inez because she wore one of those sticky name tags with her name on it.

"Hello," she said cheerfully. "Are you here for this afternoon's bingo?"

Gibson unzipped his coat and smiled. "Ahh, no ma'am. I'm a reporter for the Missoulian newspaper and I am looking for a gentleman who might live in this area." He handed her his card.

She looked at it carefully and then set it on the desk as if it might be something she did not want to touch. "Well, I know just about everybody who lives here, even some of the snowbirds. Is there some kind of trouble?"

Gibson smiled, knowing every little town in Montana had someone like Inez, someone who knew something about most of the people in their area. "No ma'am. I'm just doing a human interest story on World War Two veterans, and I was told there was one who lived near here who had quite a history. Would you happen to know who that might be?"

She thought for a moment. "Well there is one gentleman that comes in once and awhile for the potluck. Don't know when I last saw him though. I heard that he was in the war and did something with airplanes. You might try him."

"That would be great, Inez. Would you happen to know where he lives?"

Inez looked around as if she did not want anyone else to hear what she had to say even though they were the only people in the room.

"Well, I'm not one to gossip," she said in a conspiratorial whisper, "but, I have driven by his house on several occasions, up on the East Fork just across from the Jennings Creek Road."

Gibson started writing in his pad. "Oh, okay. I know where Jennings Creek is. Have not been up there in years."

"Well, the log house right across the street with the big plane propeller sticking out of the front yard? That's the place."

Gibson stood back and laughed. "My gosh, I remember seeing that years ago. Wow, you're right, Inez. There is a big propeller sticking out of the ground right in the front yard."

Inez shook her head. "Craziest thing I ever saw. Who would put something like that in their front yard anyway?"

Gibson closed his book and zipped up his jacket. "Well, Inez, that is someone I think I need to talk to. Thank you for your help."

Inez smiled. "Well, if you change your mind about bingo, we start at five. There are door prizes."

"Thank you, Inez. Maybe next time."

As he got into his truck, he thought back to the first time he saw the big grey three-blade prop sticking out of the ground. He had taken Carla, his wife, up the trail years ago so she could take photos of the area for her photography class at the university. At the time he would have done anything to please her, and he had thought doing something she wanted to do would make her happy. The two things he remembered about that trip: it didn't make her happy (she still filed for divorce the following spring) and that big grey prop sticking out of the ground.

A half hour later, a light rain that would soon turn to sleet started to fall as he slowly eased his truck past the split rail fence and turned into the narrow gravel driveway of the log home, the home with the big grey prop sticking out of the ground. It was just like he remembered. Now seeing it up close, it looked like a memorial of sorts.

As he turned off the truck, he thought of the fact that people living this far out lived in remote areas for reasons. One of them was to avoid being bothered by strangers asking personal questions. He would have to handle this carefully or risk being shown the door.. or worse.

A sudden tap on the driver's side window nearly gave him a heart attack. An old man, well into his eighties, stood near the door wearing one of those old style plaid-hunting caps with the earflaps.

Gibson rolled down the window. "You surprised me. Didn't see you walk up."

The man smiled. "Didn't mean to scare you, young man. What can I do for you?"

Gibson unlocked his door. "Do you mind if I get out? I can explain myself."

The old man held his cane against the door and smiled. "Tell ya what, young fella, why don't you stay right there and, if I like what you have to say, then you can step out. How about that? Hell, for all I know, you may be one of those people who robs old folks. I don't think I want to get robbed today."

Gibson laughed. "No, sir, I'm a reporter. I work for the paper in Missoula. Here's my card. My name is Gibson, Cliff Gibson." He stuck his hand through the window to shake.

The old man read the card and then stuck it into a worn coat pocket, a look of confusion crossing his face. He shook hands through the window but kept his cane against the door. "Okay, Cliff, why are you interested in seeing me? Am I in some kind of trouble?"

Gibson smiled. "No, sir. I just heard that you may have served in World War Two. We are doing a Veterans' Day story on local vets. That's all."

The old man thought for a moment then, asked a strange question. "How big a story you looking for?" he asked smiling. "Because if you have the time, I think I'm ready to tell a good one."

Gibson studied the old man's face looking for the joke. "I'm not sure what you mean, sir."

The old man stepped back from the door. "Tell you what, Cliff, I need a cup of coffee and I bet you do too. Let's go in the house and talk. I'm about froze."

Gibson smiled, stepped out of the truck, and followed the old man to the wide porch stairs. "Ah sir, I did not get your name. I think that might be important for the story."

The old man turned and smiled as the rain turned to a light snow. "Reynolds, Pendleton Reynolds. You can call me Penny."

For the next three hours, Penny laid out the story of his life, from the lightning strike to the Airborne program. He told about the Smoke Jumper program and even the shooting on the train. He told it all.

After filling page after page, writing as fast as he could, Gibson looked up from his notebook. "You do know, Penny, there's no statute of limitation on murder. I guess you could still be charged, even after all these years."

Penny thought for a moment. "Well, I guess that will be up to the authorities. I am ready to tell my side of it."

Gibson shook his head. "You were just a kid, Penny. I think you've already been through enough and I expect they would see it the same way."

Penny nodded and raised his cup. "I'll just have to trust your judgment on that, Cliff but I'm not sure God sees it that way."

Gibson cleared his throat. "So, you were decorated for what happened on the plane over North Africa?" he asked, changing the subject.

Penny smiled. "At first I thought I was going to be court-martialed, but twelve of the eighteen men on that plane that night survived and they ended up testifying on my behalf."

Gibson looked up from his pad. "Whatever happened to the officer you threw out of the plane? What about the pilot? Do you know where the plane ended up coming down?"

Penny thought for a moment, the memory of that night clouding his emotions. "Neither was ever found. The pilot and the Lieutenant are still listed as missing in action." His voice was barely a whisper. "One of my many regrets."

He slowly got out of his chair and retrieved a small wooden box from a shelf on the wall. As if he were holding a rare jewel, he handed Gibson the box and, with some effort, moved back to his chair and sat down.

Gibson opened it and carefully pulled up the dark blue ribbon lanyard holding the Distinguished Service Cross. A Purple Heart medal, a neatly folded letter, and two pair of silver army parachute wings were also in the box.

"Now, before I let you read that letter," announced Penny, "You need to know that I never fired a shot in the war. I only killed one man in my life and I was sixteen years old when I did it. After I was wounded, they sent me back home on a hospital ship. It took two weeks to get me back here. They found out that the bullet that went through my shoulder did damage to my heart and I was discharged in the summer of nineteen forty-three. I've been in Montana ever since."

Gibson pulled the letter from the box. "You want me to read this letter now?"

Penny nodded. "I certainly do. I think you will be surprised. Of all the things I have done in my life, it's of this that I am most proud."

Gibson set the box of medals down on the coffee table and carefully unfolded the letter. He put reading glasses back on and began to read, the snow outside beginning to fall in earnest.

Dear Mister Reynolds,

It has taken me many years to finally locate you and to be able to describe the depth of my emotions and salutations.

Through the help of my grandson and his wife, we were able to review military records and troop manifests for the American Army during the North African campaign, in particular the Allied mission designated Operation Torch. You see, Mister Reynolds, I was a young German soldier in the SS at the time and was in the battle at the airfield in Orman.

My name is Hans Minor, and you were the American soldier who captured me on the field that day, November 9th, 1942. You are the man I shot and, found out later, gravely wounded.

This letter is an account of my life and a grateful message letting you know that because you chose not to shoot me on the spot that day I survived the war and was able to live a normal life. You showed me mercy that I would not have shown you given similar circumstances. I was not the man then that I am now.

After my capture, I was turned over to American forces and spent three years in the Owasso, Michigan, Internment Camp. I was released in nineteen forty-five and returned to Germany where I have lived ever since. I am married with five grown children and seven grandchildren and will soon be a great grandfather. On my return, I worked hard and became a successful businessman, owning and then retiring from a small company that employs several hundred people.

I want you to know that, because you spared my life, many people have come into this world and, I hope made it a better place. I have you to thank for that. I lost a good friend and fellow soldier on that day, but it is my fervent hope that I have gained another with this letter.

Thank you again for my life and that of my children. I wish you continued health.

Most Sincerely,

Hans Minor

16 OBERSTAUSSE DR, APT# 8, BERLIN, GERMANY

July 14,1989

Gibson folded the letter and carefully placed it back in the box. "Have you ever made contact with Mister Minor?" he asked, still stunned by what he had just read.

Penny smiled, his eyes on some distant memory. "After my Helen died in ninety-eight, I actually went to Berlin on vacation and looked him up."

Gibson shook his head. "Jesus. What was that like? What did you say to each other?"

Penny thought for a moment, "Oh, it was a bit awkward at first," he replied sipping his coffee. "But after a few German beers, we were able to talk about the war and what kind of men we were on that day."

Gibson shook his head. "Are you still in contact with him? Did Hans talk much about what he did in the SS?"

Penny smiled. "Yes, we talk on a regular basis. As far as what he did in the SS, I know that he is still haunted by his part during the period of time he was in the unit. Like me, I think he is a man of many regrets." He bent over and put another small log in the wood stove. "I'm not his judge. Men do terrible things in war, Cliff. That's why anybody who has ever gone to war never wants to see another. As far as our communication goes," he said smiling, "Our grandchildren have taught us how to Skype. It's an amazing world, isn't it?"

As the snow continued to fall, both men sat, each in deep thought, listening to the wood stove snap and pop. Incredible things had been said and read, and much needed to be digested - an amazing story indeed.

Epilogue:

It would be well past midnight when Gibson said his goodbyes and finally made his way home to Missoula. By the time he had reached the halfway point down the mountain, he had decided what he was going to do with Penny's amazing story. He smiled, remembering the old man's last words as he walked out onto the snow-covered porch. "I never thought I would get this old." He said it with a kind of sad resolve and a look in the eye that, to a casual observer, announced that he had gotten away with something of great value - something he didn't feel he deserved.

The incredible life of one man, from the hard edge of the Depression to the desert battlefields of North Africa, was not just a story of hardship and loss, but also one of courage, perseverance, and the magnificence of the human spirit. As he crawled into bed that night, he hoped he would have been the same kind of man that Penny had been in those same situations.

He wondered if he would have been one that held the course, doing the right thing, obeying the better angels of man's nature. Maybe, but then again, men like Penny were rare, a breed apart from most, coming from a world and a time that can never be duplicated during an incredible part of our history.

Between the soft edges of coherent thought and sleep, the sound of distant thunder rolled across the night sky, a proper ending to a day of insight and inspiration. It was then that he thought of the title of the book he would start writing the next day - **To Hear Thunder.** Yeah, that would work.

In the end, it's not the years in your life that count. It's the life in your years. Abraham Lincoln

The End

This Book is dedicated to the quiet warrior. You know who you are…..and that is enough.